THE FOSSIL

THE COMPLETE NOVELLA

BY
GREIG BECK

SEVERED PRESS
HOBART TASMANIA

THE FOSSIL

Copyright © 2019 GREIG BECK

WWW.SEVEREDPRESS.COM

ISBN: 978-1-925840-60-5

There is life on other worlds.
But it is not alien.
Instead it is us, looking back from the future.

ACKNOWLEDGEMENTS:

Special mention to the 3 brave souls who offered to be my test pilots for the raw version of this upgraded novella. Thank you to Angela Johnson, Sam Stephens, and Debra Trayler.

CHAPTER 01

NEANDERS VALLEY, GERMANY 48,000 BC

Drun staggered, the skin on his upper body raw and weeping where it had been burned away. The pain was like nothing he had ever felt before in his long and arduous thirty-five years of life.

He needed to rest, he needed to hide, and he needed to find the Drawing Cave. For days, he and his tribe had been aware of the strange newcomers in their territory. He had urged his people to ignore them and simply wait until they passed on, as they had done many times before. But Orlak, Orlak the Angry One, had managed to convince the young warriors to attack them, steal their goods, and let all the peoples of other tribes know that this land belonged to the Urdan.

Drun had argued, but no one listened to the old chief anymore. Orlak carried the spear of leadership now. Only his voice would be heard.

They had crept closer to the strangers. Just like on any other hunt, they stalked their quarry; creeping forward on toes, belly-crawling through the coarse grasses, and then finally the small groups of warriors were gathered behind a stand of trees, a tumble of rocks, or just laying on their bellies, waiting for the call to attack.

They could see there were only two of the strange visitor creatures, and they were weak and so small they were tinier than the youngest child in their clan. It should have been easy—two quick kills for Orlak to crow about, and two trophies to bring back to the clan.

Orlak was first, as always, leading the tribe in a whooping charge that had surprised the pair of visitors. Before they could even react, spears were thrust into the shimmering body of one, making him collapse at their feet. But the other was faster and had not fled as they expected, instead turning to point some small object at them that flared like the brightest dayshine in its hand.

Immediately most of the tribe had been covered with fire and light, including Drun. He whimpered as he remembered the pain of the burning rays—it was like staring into the sky at the great ball of heat and fire. His eyes still ached.

Orlak had been first to be touched, and so was first to feel the sting of it. He simply vanished in the beams of light that had flown from the stranger's hand. Many of the Urdan had burned along with their new leader, their screams of fear cut off as they were turned to ash, or parts of their bodies were there one moment, and then after the light had touched them, were there no more.

They fell, their faces a mix of agony and surprise. Drun had been close, but partly shielded by the body of one of the younger warriors. Even so, the heat had been unbearable, and it had seared his flesh deeply.

In the pain and confusion, Drun was thrown to the ground and saw that the fallen visitor lay beside him with its strange belongings scattered around him. And there it was —the beautiful shiny thing. Drun had acted on instinct and snatched up the gleaming object, turning to flee.

The old warrior staggered on, finally spotting the refuge he sought. It was the deep cave they used to capture the spirits of animals they would hunt by painting their images on the walls. Drun himself had drawn bison, musk ox, and the greatest prize of all, the giant mammoth.

He crawled deep inside, the precious thing still held tight in his hand, and he dropped down against the cave wall. He grimaced as another wave of pain wracked his body. He breathed deeply for a few moments, trying to ease himself into a more comfortable position, and rested his head against the cool damp stone. He listened for the sound of pursuit, or some other beast that might have taken up residence deeper in the cave. But there was nothing, save the continual drip of milky water.

Drun opened his hand to examine the mysterious object—it was as hard as a piece of stone, but so polished and smooth it defied belief. And now when he looked closely, he could see there was something bright inside it. Something like a tiny speck of fire.

He held it in one open hand, pressing and stroking it with a blunt finger. Immediately a beam of lightning shot from its narrow end, striking the ceiling of the cave. Rocks fell, dust rose, and the small vestiges of light from outside were immediately shut out.

Drun cried aloud and his hand locked tight again over the object. Before the dust had even settled, he knew he was trapped. He cried out again but the echo of his voice was absolute. He knew then he was sealed in.

The old warrior wept; sorry for himself, sorry

for his lost brother warriors, and sorry for not being strong enough to stop Orlak from making war on the strange visitors.

He lay back, feeling again the rawness of his agonizing wounds and not caring about the constant drip of the water that fell upon his matted hair. In fact, he welcomed its coolness as it calmed the angry red burns covering his head and body.

Drun closed his eyes and let his mind wander, taking him away from the darkness and the pain. He dreamed of his youth, of his mate, of hunting in warm spring sunshine. He exhaled, the long breath leaving him slowly for the last time.

His hand stayed locked around the gleaming object as the water continued to drip down upon him.

CHAPTER 02

NEANDERS VALLEY, GERMANY – Today

Klaus Hoffman strode up the steep hill and stopped at the tree line. He used a forearm to wipe his brow and turned to look back down the slope as he waited for his girlfriend, Doris Sömmer, to catch up.

She came slowly, even though he had been carrying her pack as well as his own for the last few miles. And she still didn't look happy.

He smiled crookedly as he watched her. They'd been dating for a few years now, and every time he thought she was the one he wanted as his life-mate and planned to ask would she marry him, she'd turn on one of her frightful moods, and if she was like that in their courting days, imagine after a few years of marriage. It made him feel uneasy and unsure of himself.

He watched her close in on him—tall, brunette, with a spray of freckles across her nose and cheeks—he sighed—cute though.

She finally made it to him and grabbed his forearm to rest. She looked up into his face, her own now beet red.

"How much farther?"

He turned about, getting his bearings by judging a few of the landmarks. "Not sure exactly, but the whisper I heard about the new sinkhole placed it around here somewhere. Might be hard to spot unless we nearly fall into it."

She groaned softly and her mouth turned down at the corners. Klaus smiled back weakly, but she lowered her brow and pointed at his chest.

"Herr Hoffman, if you've dragged me up here for nothing, there'll be hell to pay."

He laughed, trying to project confidence and patted her hand. "Don't worry, we'll find it. It'll be really cool." He hoped.

Bottom line was that the geology of the area was predominantly limestone strata and therefore riddled with caves. And if a new sinkhole suddenly appeared, it meant there was a cave down there whose ceiling had collapsed. And a whole new cave meant the potential for seeing or finding something that no one else had seen before.

It was around here, Klaus was sure of it. He just needed to find it, and before anyone else. But he knew if he dragged Doris further up the slope and they found nothing, she'd be pissed off for days.

He looked about—it was a nice spot. Where they were was an easy rising slope amongst a rich green mantle of beech, hornbeam, and ravine forest trees providing a gentle cover from the sunshine.

"Why don't you sit here in the shade, and I'll do a quick scout? That way if I find something I'll shout, but if not, you won't have wasted any time."

"That's a good idea." She turned and sat on a small lump of stone, and pulled a pack of cigarettes from her pocket.

Klaus grimaced. He hated that she still smoked, at any time. But he could never understand why anyone would want to suck burning gases into their lungs when they were out in the middle of such a pristine area.

"I really want to come with you." She reached out and grabbed his hand.

He smiled down at her, knowing she didn't mean it. Doris was definitely a work in progress, and he couldn't help loving her—most of the time.

"Back soon."

Klaus turned and bounded up the hill. Most of the Neander Valley had been heavily quarried for the limestone over the previous century, but today it had been allowed to regrow, renew, and return to its once pre-industrialized, pre-modern human state.

Though the quarrying had been a boon to the local area for jobs and money, for future fossil hunters, the downside of the heavy mining was that it left few caves—even the famous one where the first Neanderthal remains were discovered had been obliterated. Therefore, he had to keep a lookout for older areas of forest, ones that signified they had never been excavated before.

He continued on, trying to cut a zigzag path while also trying to remember his landmarks to find his way back. As he ventured on, the surrounding trees became older, more gnarled, and on the ground were logs that were rotted down over the many decades.

"Around here somewhere," he whispered and leapt up one of the fallen boughs, to slowly turn his head.

"There." He grinned. He could see two trees that were bent at odd angles—leaning toward each other as though curtseying before a dance.

He leapt down and jogged toward them,

slowing as he came closer. His smile spread across his face; there was a dark hole in the ground and there were trees, still green, sticking up from it that had obviously just toppled in. *Perfect*, he thought, as they also made ideal ladders.

He quickly spun about making note of the trees, rocks, and landscape to mark his place, and then turned to rush back to where he had left Doris.

He always felt he had to struggle to impress her, but there was no way this was going to fail to blow her mind.

*****

"Phew." Doris covered her nose.

"Just a little bit of stale air." Klaus sniffed deeply. "But not too bad. In fact, that's a good sign. Means this cave has been totally sealed up for a long time." He slowly looked around. "And I'm guessing for years, maybe even tens of thousands of years."

They were still under the halo of light afforded by the sinkhole opening above them, and Klaus drew out his large flashlight. He shone it around, seeing the dark passage yawning before him.

"That way." He looked over his shoulder.

"Gonna be totally dark the further in we go, so we're going to need your light as well. Hurry and get it out and let's go."

"I haven't got it," she muttered.

"What?" He fully turned. "I left you the big red one, the best one, remember?"

She shook her head. "It was too heavy."

He straightened, bumping his head on a hanging tree root. "So you just left it behind?"

"I didn't think I'd need it." She shrugged. "Besides, I can't carry *everything*."

"O-*oookay*." He turned back to the ink-black cave passage. "Just stay close to me then."

He guided her in, and as they moved further away from the light, it got as dark as he expected and even more claustrophobic. It didn't bother Klaus as he loved cave exploring, and especially fossil hunting. He wasn't so sure about Doris as he felt her hand on his jacket, scrunching the material up into a tight ball.

They edged along, sometimes having to bend forward to navigate the tighter spots, and soon came to an area that opened out. Klaus straightened, panning his light around.

"Wow! Do you see?"

There were drawings all around them, and their detail was magnificent—giant bison, antelope, and even the huge mammoth.

"It's beautiful," Doris said.

"I know." He grinned and grabbed her hand, squeezing it. "And we're the first people to see it in thousands and thousands of years."

"They were good artists…especially for cavemen," she declared.

"They sure were. And they didn't do it just for the aesthetics. It's thought that they believed that by reproducing the animal's images on the walls, they also captured the beast's souls. Then it gave them the beast's power during the hunt."

She snorted, still looking around for another moment, before turning back to him. "Now what?"

"Now what?" he repeated and sighed.

From up ahead something glinted back at them, and he craned his neck forward. "Come on." He tugged her forward and came to a bulge in the cave wall. He frowned, squinting in at it.

"Hey, there's something in there."

Klaus Hoffman shone his flashlight onto the wall of the new cave, moving it slowly back and forth, letting the beam penetrate from different angles. He felt rather than heard Doris creep closer.

"What?" She then sniffed in the cold darkness, letting him know her disinterest was peaking again.

"Look, look." He turned and grabbed her sleeve as he crouched down, pulling her toward him.

"*Ow*." Doris pulled her arm away from his grasp. He'd thought his girlfriend had been slightly interested in entering the cave. He couldn't count the times she had seemed to sit spellbound as he had recounted his many spelunking adventures over the past few months. Perhaps her interest had been feigned, or perhaps her interest only extended to hearing about caves—entering them was a whole different ballgame.

"I don't see anything." She looked away and down into the interior of the cave. "It's too dark. And wet. And cold." She sniffed again. "And smells funny."

Klaus muttered in annoyance and tugged her sleeve again. "Here...don't look *at* the rock, look into it. It's called a limestone flow, and it's rather like solidified dishwater...cloudy but you can still see through it."

She had folded her arms, leaned forward, and craned her neck. But after a few seconds, she slowly shook her head. "Nope, nothing."

Klaus started to groan in frustration and then had a thought. He held up a finger and then fumbled under his jacket for his water bottle, uncapped it, and splashed the liquid onto the bulge in the cave wall. The smooth limestone now revealed looked more like glistening wax. He smiled and sat back on his haunches.

"The flow is the result of tens of thousands of years of water dripping down to coat everything in micro-mineral particles. It eventually hardens to a semi-clear covering. It's the geological equivalent of capturing prehistoric bugs in amber." Klaus changed the angle of his light beam once again. "Now look."

"Oh yeah, I can see inside—*yuck*—that thing looks weird." Doris wrinkled her nose but crouched beside him.

"Looks beautiful to me." Klaus tipped some more water over it and wiped a hand over the smooth lump of milky stone.

"Is it a man? He looks deformed or something." Doris got to her feet to change angles, and he liked that she kept her hand on his shoulder as she stared into the wet stone.

"You mean, *was*. And no, I don't think he was deformed. Judging by the depth of mineral coverage, I'd say he's been trapped in there for at least forty to fifty thousand years, maybe even sixty thousand." Klaus leaned in, his nose almost touching the slick stone. "Not deformed, more like proto-human...probably Neanderthal."

He shone his torch at the cave wall and ceiling before letting it rest on her face. "The sinkhole we entered only opened the cave a couple of days back, and so far the only people who know about it are you, me, and a few disinterested locals. We're probably the first people to set foot in here for tens of thousands of years." He raised his eyebrows theatrically.

Her eyes went from him to the stone. "So us finding it means we own it?"

"Well, not really; it's not our land." He bobbed his head. "But...it is *our* find. So we can claim naming rights."

Doris scoffed. "Ooh, you'll be rich."

"Maybe just famous in the fossil-hunting magazines." He grinned up at her.

She just nodded but with little enthusiasm. Klaus shrugged, still feeling the tingle of excitement ripple through him. He turned back to lean in close again, inhaling the smell of the ancient stone. He could smell the age of the rock and it made him tingle all over.

From behind there came the sound of a metallic flicking, followed by a spark of light.

He spun. "Doris! Are you shitting me...you're

smoking?"

She pointed the cigarette at him like the barrel of a small glowing gun. "I'm nervous. You know I smoke when I'm nervous. I'm nervous, cold, hungry…and horny." She tilted her nose in the air, but looked back at him out of the corner of her eye.

Klaus snorted. He knew when she threw in the horny angle she wanted to distract him, or simply change the subject. Normally, she got her way, but this time, his focus remained firmly above his waistline. This was way too important.

"Hey, you smoke when you're nervous, drunk, happy, sad…face it, Doris, you smoke all the time. Show some respect; this cave probably hasn't seen people for about fifty thousand years…and do you mind not dropping ash everywhere?"

She wobbled her head. "I've seen you smoke too, Mr. High-n-mighty. Besides, who's going to complain…him?" She jerked her thumb at the lump in the wall, jammed the cigarette between her pursed lips, and flashed a quick glance at the blue Seiko dive watch on her slim wrist.

Klaus ignored her and looked back at the encased body. A thought began to form in his mind. "Maybe…and for the record, for all we know, it might be a her."

He dug a thumbnail into the flowstone and

managed to pick a small piece of the soft rock away. "We need to dig it out—looks really old and if it's a good quality fossil, which I think it is, it could be worth thousands." He half turned. "And the smoke could damage it."

"Thousands." Klaus heard her softly repeat the word, and then came the sound of a foot grinding something into the cave floor.

He nodded sagely. "Sure, collectors pay a fortune for this stuff. They'll even pay for pieces of it. Limestone flows are very soft. We need to get some tools and cut it out before anyone else finds this cave. After all, vandals could destroy it, right?"

Doris crowded in beside him, squinting. "Good idea." She pointed. "Hey, I think there's a light in there."

He followed her finger. "*Hmm*, might be a reflection—or an opal. Could make it even more valuable." He straightened. "One thing's for sure: I'm getting it out."

CHAPTER 03

NEW BERLIN, GERMANIA, 50,000 AD

"Let's go, let's go, let's go." Jax slapped each soldier on the back as they jogged past—twenty of the best combat professionals and genetically bred to be big, tough, and fearless. Zone-Cleaners, ass-kickers, terminators, call them whatever you wanted, but they got the job done, and the harder and dirtier, the better. Jax was satisfied; he had his war party, and they were ready to kick ass.

The portal flared as they all lined up to one side, awaiting his final inspection. Nano body-armor over iron-hard muscles, fusion bombs, magnetic kill-darts, and burners with enough power to fry a city block. He walked along the line, nodding to each, their eyes straight ahead.

He balled a fist, holding it up as he faced them. "We are the hammer, and they are the nail.

When we strike, they fall. We will not fail…we *cannot* fail." He raised the fist higher, his jaw jutting. "Anything gets in our way, it's dead." Jax began to turn away, but paused, his head tilting. He spun back and roared. *"I can't… fucking… hear you."*

As one, the squad yelled in return: "Anything in our way is dead."

The squad leader grinned without humor. "Damned right." He turned to the glowing portal. "Let's go and scare the shit out of some Monst."

He turned his back on them and waited for the portal to open fully and settle itself. He felt the familiar tingling in his belly as the atmospheric ionization distorted the molecules in the air right in front of him.

Time-travel had been discovered by accident in a physics laboratory over a thousand years ago. Who would have thought that the most powerful weapon the world had ever seen started out on a holo-board, created by some chinless nerd in a stained shirt.

Of course, it had immediately been commandeered by the military. Something so powerful and dangerous could never be allowed into the hands of their enemies, or even worse, the people.

And though it was heavily controlled and regulated, accidents still happened—they'd all been educated on what occurred when you played around with the past; all sorts of crazy shit started going down.

And when the inevitable fuck-ups did happen, well, that's where Jax and his Time-Cleaners came in.

Jax rolled his shoulders and drew in a breath. The zone they were about to enter was dangerous. The Monst had evolved, changed, become clever and far more deadly.

Jax was the senior officer in charge of the top cleanup crew, and he was fearless. He knew his men would follow him to Hell if need be…and that was good, because where they were going *was* Hell, and there were demons living there—the Monst—monsters from the dark times of prehistory that defied belief.

All record of them had been obliterated during the great war of 3020AD. Everything had been burned to ash, and by the time they rose again from those cinders, the monsters had retreated to become myths, legends, and stories only told to children to scare them at night.

Then the test pilots, the first jumpers, went back through a portal, and they saw them. Jax laughed; he would have loved to have seen the look on that very first sucker's face as he stepped out of the portal and looked up into the maw of one of those freaking monsters.

Jax breathed deeply and cast his mind back to how they had got to this point. His lips moved in a silent curse: *damn science officers and their weak-willed approach to everything*. He was sick of hearing their advice given to Command: "We don't need to take any Zone-Cleaners on jumps; the Monst fear us more than we fear them; we must hold out the hand of peace." *Ha*, he thought with a little vindication. Hold out the "hand of peace" and you'd fucking lose it. As the science team had just found out…yet again.

Jax snorted as he checked his burner's power cells. Gilbred, that worm, and his know-it-all colleague Hindoy, now deceased, had found out the hard way exactly what happened when you got lazy, inattentive, or just plain stupid. He remembered when the puny excuse for a Germanian had returned from his expedition, shaking like a leaf.

He glanced at the chronometer. The portal's synchronizers had identified their destination and started the countdown.

Thirty…twenty-nine…twenty-eight…twenty-seven...

"On my six," he yelled over his shoulder as the seconds vanished.

There'd been too many trips now. They had burned, interrogated, and tortured their way across a lot of the primordial hellhole to get to this point. Now, it all came down to this last zone jump.

As he waited for the portal to stabilize, he let his mind wander over the events of the past few days. Back to Gilbred and when he had first returned from his fateful trip.

*****

Jax lunged forward and yelled into the seated science officer's face. "You fucking lost it? You get attacked by a few dumb Monst, let them creep right up on you, and spear Hindoy? Then you let them take his damn burner?"

Jax paced, his jaw clenched. He spun back. "You upbraid my soldiers for stepping on a single bug, but in a blind panic you fry ten Monst." Jax rushed back, getting in close to the cowering scientist. "Do you have any idea what sort of problems this will cause?" He brought his face so close to Gilbred's that their foreheads almost touched. "Well?"

Gilbred squeaked something incomprehensible. Jax stepped around the science officer, his lips tight in barely suppressed fury. He stopped behind the man and leaned in close to seethe into his ear. "If you had left his body behind, I'd damn well make sure you spend a week in a pain chamber...of my choosing." Jax straightened, his hands clasped behind his back, chin lifted. "Why do you science guys always think you know what's best?"

Gilbred shook his head. "We knew the Monst were in the area, but they had been so docile before. We didn't think they'd..." His voice, already high and strained from fear, trailed off as Jax turned, a scowl pulling his face into deep fissures.

Gilbred hung his head. Jax smiled and patted the man's shoulder. "You didn't think. Don't worry. That's what we do...and that's why we told you we needed to accompany you on your jumps." He snorted. "But you knew better." Jax growled. "Yes, you brainy types *always* know better."

Gilbred lifted his head. "I can help you to—"

Jax's voice was so loud Gilbred nearly fell out of his chair. "Shut the fuck up; you've done enough already." He exhaled loudly. "The burners do not corrode, erode, or malfunction—we designed them that way. That thing will be in operation for a quarter of a million years."

He sighed and placed both hands on Gilbred's narrow shoulders, leaning in close to his other ear. "Do you know what will happen if those Monst get that technology? Next time we drop in on them, they'll fry us." Jax pushed back off the man and walked around in front of him.

"We need to find it." He stopped and stared down at the cowering man. "*You* need to find it. We can't go back to the same zone twice because of the paradox whiteout, so you need to locate the lost burner's xenon radiation trace and then follow it back up the event slope. Give me a place and a date, and we'll go get it ourselves."

Jax's voice became soft. "A warning, though. Make sure you're accurate. It costs a small fortune to open those portals, so we better locate it before the general finds out." He turned slowly. "Because you think I'm scary? Just wait until *he's* in your face."

Jax nodded to the door. "Get out."

CHAPTER 04

BERLIN, MARZAHN, SOCIAL HOUSING DISTRICT

Doris sat in the armchair and let another cigarette butt fall to the floor. *Was it her 10th for the day, 20th, 30th?* It didn't matter anymore. Nothing mattered anymore.

She slowly placed her foot on the still-glowing butt to grind it out on the mold- and piss-smelling carpet. Her eyes were dark-ringed, and just in the last few weeks she had lost so much weight her cheeks had hollowed out.

Not sleeping hadn't helped either. Every time she tried to shut her eyes she heard them moving in the walls—always watching, always present. They weren't the neighbors, or even rats, or possums, or birds; that she knew. They were something else entirely.

She punched down hard on her thigh: *fuck Klaus, fuck, fuck, fuck him and his stupid fossils. That's when it all started.* She wished she hadn't gone into that dirty cave, or picked up that weird thing, and right now, she wished she had never met him.

Her eyes darted to the other wall, and she felt a tear run down her cheek. She needed him bad. And she was so scared she couldn't think straight.

He had said he was going to find someone to help them, but she hadn't seen or heard from him in days. In turn, she was stuck in this horrible rent-by-the-night apartment, chosen because it was anonymous, secretive, and available. And she was all alone.

Her eyes flicked to the wall again. Almost alone.

She continued to stare at the flaking wall. Once she had placed an ear to it and heard them whispering. She couldn't make out what they were saying, but she was sure it was words, and she was also sure it wasn't her damned crack-head neighbors.

She heard a noise that sounded like a cross between bacon frying and electricity crackling coming from her bedroom. Doris slowly turned to the closed door. She sniffed, smelling something that was sharp, acrid, and left a weird metallic taste in the back of her mouth. She swallowed it down in a dry throat and stared so hard at the door it made her head ache.

"Fuck off!" she screamed.

The door handle slowly started to turn.

"*Oh God*," she breathed.

CHAPTER 05

NEW BERLIN, GERMANIA – RECOVERY
MISSION

Jax was first through the portal. The chronometer
indicated the signature radiation traces had
appeared again; many millennia after Gilbred had
lost his weapon, and in a time and place they were
loath to visit.

It meant the burner had been released from
wherever it had been sealed off from the open air
and hidden from the scans. But there was a further
complication in that there were many traces
showing. Somehow, the burner had infused objects
around it with the xenon particles, and now they
were spread over a large area. And that meant the
team had to check every damn one of them.

Jax was confident his cleanup crew was a
good one—tough and brutal, and all professional

zone-jump soldiers. He knew they'd need to be. Coming to this type of zone was not recommended. It was too dangerous. The Monst had evolved a base intelligence, a hunter's smarts to add to their monstrous muscle power.

He stepped into the dark space, only just remembering in time to snap his faceplate down. The air was foul, and the gasses would quickly sear his lungs. Only the giant Monst, with their enormous bellow-like breather bags, could absorb the mix of primordial gases.

He looked around. *So damn big*, he thought. Even though he was a veteran of the race wars, the class wars, and gender wars, and as battle-hardened as they come, these creatures scared the shit out of him. Each stood over three times as tall as his biggest man, and most Monst could literally tear him or his soldiers to pieces with their bare hands.

Jax circled his finger in the air and his team started their search. There were familiar radiation vestiges, but they were faint—the burner had been here at some time. His team examined, probed, and searched their way across the dark expanse where the initial trace was detected.

It only took them a few minutes to return empty—nothing on scanners, nothing on visual.

Arcad, his lead Cleaner, shrugged. "Not here. Might have been once, but not now. What do you want to do, boss?"

Jax thought for a moment. "Broaden the search area. If it's not here, I want to know what happened to it. Let's do a quick check in the outer areas."

"Outer areas?" Arcad's head snapped up. "There are indications of current habitation."

"That's right, soldier...and that's why they pay us the big glots." Jax grinned and moved to the entrance of the large space. He slowed, holding up one hand as he heard a sound from outside. He and the team froze.

Arcad eased up next to him. "Go or no go?" He looked over his shoulder to the portal gateway shimmering in the darkness behind them.

Jax continued to hold up a hand as he waited, listening. He placed his ear to the entrance and then shook his head. "Nothing." He half turned to his second-in-command. "I don't like it either, but we've already done the jump and we're here to do a job. So, we do it thoroughly."

Besides, he thought, one of the anomalies in the temporal paradox meant they couldn't come back to this time spot even if they wanted to. If they missed something, then it was just too bad.

He wasn't a tech-head, but it had something to do with cataclysmic temporal atom stacking. Seems the universe didn't like it when you ran into an earlier or later version of yourself—it happened once, before Jax was recruited, and the effects were catastrophic. A team of scientists had jumped back to 1908, Tunguska in Siberia. And then jumped back again to finish their work. Unfortunately, they had their jump calibrations off by 12 seconds, and ran smack into themselves— the result? Their atoms exploded, devastating 700 square miles of frozen forest.

If that had happened in a major city, there was no amount of cleaning that would wash that off the timeline.

Jax steeled himself and then reached up and grabbed the opening lever.

"Lend a hand here, soldier."

Arcad stepped forward and also took hold of the lever and together they pulled the huge barrier back toward them. It opened easily, with only a faint whine of protest.

Jax was first through as always, leading by example, with his team quickly in behind him. Jax was the most skilled Cleaner in Germania and as soon as he orientated himself, he knew there was danger. He sensed rather than saw the Monst as it leapt up to loom over them.

The sound that smashed out of the darkness made them all want to cover their ears and flee. The great beast's maw was open, a near perfect circle, and huge teeth framed the ear-shattering screech that smashed at them like a physical force.

Jax had encountered them before, but in the past, he and his teams had always tried to stay out of sight. Now being caught out in the open and having one tower over him like a mountain of flesh, teeth, and muscle, made the iron-hard soldier feel a slight tremble in his knees.

The Monst raised one colossal arm and took a single ground-shaking step. Jax didn't wait to see if it held something dangerous as his training took over. He lifted his burner, set to wide beam, and fired. The beast shimmered for a moment or two as the beam struck it and the sound of its terrifying call immediately shut off as it disintegrated.

"Shit, shit, shit." He had no choice. The Time Displacement nerds hated to see Monst removed from this zone as they had strong social bonding. *Too late now*, he thought.

"We need to move quickly. Give me a thorough search, and then let's get the hell out of here." He bristled. Those assholes back home better find him the right zone next time, or he'd personally feed them all to the Monst.

It took them only a few more minutes to confirm there was no sign of their missing burner. Jax herded his team back to the portal, taking one last look around. He took a few more seconds to seal the entrance and make sure he had left no evidence from his team. The other creatures would find the remains of the giant beast soon enough, but as long as the crew wasn't seen, the Monst would be as clueless as always. *Primitives,* he thought.

He bared his teeth and growled at the waste of money, waste of effort, and a waste of fucking time.

"And no burner," he spat back at the empty room.

Jax stepped back through the glowing portal and it immediately snapped shut behind him. The surroundings rapidly cooled, and silence settled once more.

CHAPTER 06

GERMANY, BERLIN – TODAY

"It's not you, it's me." Johanna had met him at their front door, barring his way with her arms folded and her eyes downcast.

"No, no." Ed reached out a hand to lay it on her forearm, but she gently eased back half a step and he let it slide away. "Honey, I'm sorry. If it's something I've done or said, or something I haven't done or said…"

She shook her beautiful blonde head.

"Well, what? I know I've been working too many late nights lately, but I can make that up to you." He brightened. "You know, I was actually saving for us to go on holiday together. Somewhere nice, maybe in the sun."

She finally looked up, but instead of interest, or sadness, or even regret, he just saw a stony resolution in her ice blue eyes, and it made his heart sink.

"It's not that, Ed." She exhaled and bobbed her head a little from side to side. "We're just…different people now."

"I'm not." He smiled, brokenly.

"Maybe I wish you were." Her mouth pressed into a tight little line for a moment, and then her jaw became set. "I'm sorry, but you need to move out." She stood aside a fraction. "I've packed your things."

His mouth dropped open when he spotted two suitcases and an overnight bag waiting for him.

"What?"

He didn't see that coming; it was all too quick. Things had gone from what he thought was unhappiness and a little distance between them to a real full-on breakup.

"What did I do? For how long?" He shook his head. "Just tell me what I did. I can make it up to you, promise." He hated begging, but… "Just give me—"

"No." She squeezed her eyes shut.

Ed reached out a hand to her again, but this time she flinched away. He suddenly had a leaden feeling in his gut, and he asked the question he couldn't avoid.

"Is there…someone else?"

She kept her head down, and after a second, a nearly imperceptible nod. Ed felt like all the color and light in his life had immediately been drained away.

"Who is it?" He sighed. "*Ah*, doesn't matter." He nodded. "Okay." He grabbed his bags and turned to walk down the few steps to his car.

He turned, trying to think of something devastatingly poignant to say to her, that she'd remember forever. But she was already closing the door, on him, and on their future.

She always said he loved his job more than her, and now it looks like the job won out. The thing was he didn't think he was all that good at that either.

Detective Ed Heisen of the Berlin Kripo—the *Kriminalpolizei*—hefted the bags and walked them to the rear of his car. He looked back to stare hard at the closed door for a moment.

While I'm working, you're fucking someone else. Thanks for nothing…and good riddance, bitch, he thought harshly.

"That's what I should have said," he muttered and threw the bags in the back of the car and slammed the trunk shut. He looked back up at their, her, window again.

"Nah, I don't mean that." He sighed, long and loud. "I'll miss you, beautiful."

CHAPTER 07

GERMANY, FRANKFURT – MANN EISEN
BAR

Monroe drank his beer and watched Raptor, his second-in-command, bring the man down over his knee. The man's backbone made a noise like a snapping tree branch.

He let the spasming body slide to the floor. Monroe knew Raptor didn't care whether his opponent walked again or died right there at his feet. Neither did Monroe.

Raptor's opponent had been big, beefy, and knew how to throw a punch. Probably won plenty of fights in his time. From the minute Monroe and Raptor had walked in through the doors, the asshole glared, sized them up, and then to the delight of his drinking buddies, decided to get in their faces.

Perhaps he thought he was going to let them know whose territory they had just walked in on. Or perhaps he had been carried away by his own alcohol-fueled bravado. Monroe told him to walk away. The asshole chose not to.

Monroe half turned to his buddy. "Raptor."

"My pleasure, boss." Raptor had gotten to his feet and on his way up, had collected an almighty uppercut under his chin. That was Beefy's last mistake.

The man was big, as big as Raptor, but where this guy had broad shoulders, log-like arms, and a chin that looked like it was carved from stubbled granite, his stomach told of a man who had let himself go. His fighting modus operandi was obviously to throw a few big bombs with stunning power and hope to end the fight quickly.

It'd probably work on someone who hadn't been biologically bred for strength, stamina, and was trained for war.

Raptor had taken a step back after the first haymaker, and then lightly ducked under the next. As Beefy's arm swung in on the follow-through, Raptor had come up and sent a pile driver right into the huge gut.

It was done with the full swing of arm and shoulder, putting all the upper body's strength into the blow. Beefy lost his breath and a good deal of his beer.

Raptor followed with a quick left and right to each side of his head. The big guy had staggered back, landing against the bar. He turned to grab a bottle and swung it at Raptor's face.

Raptor easily caught his wrist, held it, and then jerked him forward to head-butt the guy's nose with a gruesome wet crunch that splashed his friends at the bar in blood and snot.

Then it was time to finish him—Raptor grabbed his shirt and pants, lifted the huge man high above his head, then swung him down using his own bodyweight across his propped knee.

The crack of backbone was sickeningly loud in the now tomb-silent bar, and Monroe grinned and shook his head. Like a victorious silver-backed gorilla, Raptor now stood like a bloody colossus over the man, looking around the bar. His shaven head, pale blue eyes that were so light they almost looked alien, plus battle-scarred face, now set him and Monroe as a breed apart from everyone else in the bar.

Both men stood six foot three and were as solid as iron from their genetic breeding and also their Special Forces training. But where Monroe was athletically long-limbed, Raptor was a human bulldozer.

Monroe pivoted his head, taking in the other barroom patrons; some of them had been drinking with the man Raptor had just brutalized. Not a single one of them now looked at either of the two men. Raptor's brutal and efficient violence had made them invisible. Even the barman had taken to polishing glasses with such concentration he looked like he was trying to work out how to split the atom.

Monroe's pocket buzzed. He frowned. It was extremely rare to get called on downtime. He and his team belonged to an internal military body simply called Defense. They operated on orders issued from a few generals, and the president himself—they didn't exist until they needed to.

He pulled the disc-reader. *Something big must be going down*, he thought. He read the message:

POSSIBLE NT INCURSION. He grunted. *NT – Non-Terrestrial*.

Monroe clicked his fingers at his soldier and headed to the exit. Raptor followed, but at the door the big man paused to look back. Not a single person looked up, their drinks now the most interesting thing in the world.

CHAPTER 08

BERLIN – KRIMINALPOLIZERI HEADQUARTERS

"Hey, Agent Fox Mulder," the large detective yelled as he came down through the crowded room, just barely fitting between the desks.

"Yeah, yeah, very funny, Schneider." Heisen swung in his seat. "What?"

Schneider stopped to look down at the food selection in the shopping bag Heisen had beside the desk.

"Dining alone?"

"For the time being." Heisen waited. "So?"

"So I heard you broke up...and Johanna is single again?" He raised his eyebrows. "Would you mind if I...?"

"You?" Heisen looked up at the overweight, slightly balding, and middle-aged Schneider, with coffee stains like a badge of honor on his right man-boobed breast. He grinned. "Not at all. Give her your best shot, buddy."

"Thank you. I always liked her." Schneider bobbed his head.

"Now that we've organized your dating schedule, what did you want?" Heisen lifted his chin.

"Oh, the boss is looking for you." He thumbed over his shoulder. "New case, Fox; right up your alley."

Heisen groaned as he got to his feet. He didn't mind the nickname of the FBI agent from the old sci-fi series, and in fact thought he looked a little like the actor. What he didn't like was being handed all the weirdest and wackiest cases in the district.

He knocked on the captain's door and waited, peering in through the glass as his senior officer was on a call. He kept talking as he waved Heisen in.

Heisen sat down and Captain Müller continued with his call, not making eye contact, but pushed a piece of paper across his desk toward him. He tapped it with one big blunt finger.

Heisen picked it up and quickly read it—it was just a name and address.

Müller put a hand over the phone speaker. "A body; sounds a little weird." He grinned and winked. "Perfect for you." He made a shooing motion with his hand. But then quickly clicked his fingers, and then placed a hand over the speaker again.

"Hey, Ed, sorry to hear about you and Johanna."

"Thank you." Heisen got to his feet.

"So she's single again?" Müller's eyebrows were up.

"Oh yeah she is…and looking to date another cop." He held up the address. "I'm on it, Chief." On his way out, he lowered his voice. "And thank you for the insightful briefing."

*****

"Victim's name is Doris Sömmer—at least we think it's her." Sergeant Artur Amos led Detective Ed Heisen through the dark, stinking apartment.

"Based on a next-to-useless imprint of the driver's license at the check-in desk, we believe we got a twenty-six-year-old female, Caucasian, approximately five-eight tall. But, fingerprints gone, weight unknown, hair and eye color also unknown."

"Unknown? I thought you said you had a body." Heisen followed the older policeman, squinting to try and improve his vision in the semi-gloom. He looked across to the windows and saw why—they had been painted over or had newspaper taped across them.

Amos half turned and shrugged. "Meh." He handed Heisen a sheet of paper with some basic background information and a copy of the girl's driver's license. A small, grainy photo just showed a healthy young woman beaming at the camera.

"What about other prints?" Heisen asked while reading the page.

"Millions of 'em," replied the short cop.

Heisen looked up as Amos slowed at the doorway to a room floodlit by halogen lamps and bustling with several shapes in white biohazard suits. Amos flipped a page from his notebook and read off more details.

"Evidence of a metallic band on the fourth ring finger indicating a possible engagement, but the diamond is gone, and there's evidence she was with someone. So we're still looking for trace." He snorted and stood aside. "And yeah, we thought we had a body too." Amos pointed with his pen.

Heisen stepped past the smaller man and looked down at the sticky carpet. There was an ash outline, almost too perfect in detail. He didn't know whether to laugh or stagger from the room screaming his head off.

"Jesus Christ! What'd they use, a freakin' blowtorch?"

The body, or what had once been a body, was just a thin layer of grey-brown ash in the shape of a figure holding an arm up, either warding off a blow or trying to shield her vision from something.

Amos pointed again with the pen. "No idea what caused it, but whatever it was, it was freaking hot. We think the ring…" he leaned forward and indicated a darker area on the end of the ash-arm pile on the carpet, "…once had a diamond. Well, we think that's what it was, as the lab boys tell me that there's a small trace of mineralized carbon ash denser than the rest."

Amos looked up at Heisen. "Do you know how hot a fire needs to be before a diamond burns?"

Heisen shook his head. "I didn't even know they could burn."

"Me neither, but I looked it up. It usually takes about fifteen hundred degrees. But this must have been even hotter and faster, 'cause if you heat man's best friend up slowly, it explodes."

"Girl's best friend," Heisen murmured.

"Man's best friend is a dog."

Amos scoffed. "Then we got the better deal. Anyways, we reckon this was a burn of about two thousand degrees, and it occurred over just a few seconds."

"That's incredible." Heisen squatted beside Amos.

The cop waved his pen around. "That's nuthin; look around, Detective." Amos swiveled his head theatrically, and then faced Heisen, his eyebrows raised.

"Nothing else is burned. The heat happened right here, right on her, *just* on her, for the blink of an eye, and then just as miraculously, it must have turned itself off. What could do that?"

Heisen grunted and looked up—the ceiling was also unharmed. He nodded. "Well, wasn't a flamethrower, that'd fry the plaster overhead, or at least leave a helluva stain."

He sniffed. There was a strange smell, but not the greasy odor he expected when a body got cooked. He'd seen people burned up before and the fact was, Joe or Jane Doe contained a good percentage of fat, women more so. Even a healthy woman carried about ten percent body fat— burning it should have filled the room with greasy smoke and the smell of fried pork. Instead, there was nothing but a sharp metallic odor.

Heisen pulled on his lower lip as he thought for a moment, and then clicked his fingers. "Microwaves."

"Huh?" Amos looked at him as if he had just started to speak in another language.

"Microwaves. You know, like what you get in a microwave oven. I hear that the military is working on some sort of device to project the waves that'll cook you from the inside out, but leaves all the buildings intact."

Amos's expression didn't soften, but his head tilted by about half a degree and one of his eyebrows went up by just as much. "Rays? Army fucking mi-cro-waves? Is that your deduction, Detective?"

Heisen half shrugged. "Well, what've you got?"

Heisen didn't really think it was caused by microwaves either, as he'd also read that the devices were as large as a good-sized refrigerator—not exactly something you'd cart up to the first floor of some back-alley flea-pit, use it to fry a young woman, and then slip out the back door with it hidden under your coat.

As Amos turned to speak to a couple of uniformed policemen, Heisen stepped back to look down at the outline again, trying to imagine how the girl had been standing before she had fallen back or been pushed to the ground. One arm was up, appearing as if she had the arm across her face at the moment of death, perhaps trying to protect herself from whatever killed her.

Heisen tried to twist himself into the right shape, with his legs splayed, one arm out, and the other over his face. He let his eyes move to a doorway on the other side of the apartment. She would have been facing that room. Whatever had killed her had come from there. The door was closed.

He reached into his pocket and felt for a small plastic sample bottle he always kept there. He could wait for Amos to release the forensic results, or he could do some of his own testing. Heisen looked over his shoulder and saw Amos signing something for a young cop—*now*, he thought. He quickly opened the bottle, scooped a tiny bit of the ash residue into it, sealed it, and placed it and his hand in his pocket as he got to his feet.

The shove to his back nearly threw him to the floor. Heisen spun to see six enormous human beings, all dressed in plain black coveralls, push into the room—five men, one woman, all with faces hard enough to put a dent in a steel door.

One calmly started giving orders, and immediately the group began to spread out, some waving strange devices, the rest joining the guys in HAZMAT suits and taking their reports from them. Heisen noticed all had powerful-looking sidearms strapped to their thighs.

"Hey, who the fuck are you guys?" Amos charged over, waving his arms, flanked by two young policemen. The senior policeman went to grab one of the men by the arm. The effect was immediate and alarming—like lightning, Amos' hand was grabbed and twisted. The senior cop screamed, and the two policemen went for the guns. But before they could even get close to drawing them, five weapons were all aimed at the police. The young cops swallowed; behind them, the technicians froze, watching. The young policeman's eyes slid to Amos.

Heisen recognized the guns—all Heckler & Koch USP Tactical. What caught his attention was the modified O-ring barrel with polygonal bore profile and taller sights for using sound suppressors. It also had a slide rail for laser sights—these were not your standard kit, even for the *Kommando Spezialkräfte*.

Time seemed to stand still for several seconds.

"Let him go," the black-clad leader said softly.

Amos was released and he rubbed his hand, looking like he couldn't decide whether he wanted to walk away or go for his own gun. The leader, and the only one who hadn't bothered pulling a weapon, touched something at his ear and spoke a few words. The cop's phone began to ring.

"Answer it," he said to Amos.

Heisen watched as Amos kept his eyes on the big man and pulled out his phone. He lifted it to his ear. "Amos." He listened, his brow folding.

He disconnected and turned to his officers. "At ease; that was the boss." He shrugged. "Actually, even further up the chain of command than the boss." He turned away, rubbing his arm. "Let these...*agents*...look around...and give them any assistance they need." Amos turned back to the man he assumed was in charge. "What's your name?" The older cop tilted his chin, waiting.

He was ignored, pushed aside, and the agents resumed going about their tasks. Heisen sidled up next to Amos. "Who the hell are these guys?"

Amos shrugged. "From Defense." He began to walk away.

"Defense? Defense what—Army, Navy, Spezialkräfte, Homeland, who?" Heisen got in front of Amos.

Amos motioned with his hand to the huge

agents. "Be my guest, Detective."

There was a woman amongst the group of special agents; Heisen would have described her as being brutally attractive, leaning a little more toward the brutally part. Not really his type, but since Johanna had thrown him out, he guessed everyone was a potential 'his type' from now on.

He straightened and also broadened his shoulders a little, and then switched on his most disarming smile as he approached.

"Hi there, I'm Ed…"

"Fuck off." She kept walking.

"And nice to meet you too." Heisen waved at her back.

He decided to watch and backed up to the wall. It seemed the mystery Defense squad were going to give them nothing. He could try again, maybe beg them for information, or he could do his own job. He moved away from the wall, knowing he only had a few minutes before these guys, whoever they were, shut them all down. If he wanted answers, he'd have to get them himself…and quick.

He stepped around the forensics guys down on their knees sifting and lifting minute bits of evidence from the carpet. As he went by, he reached down to lift a rubber glove from one of their cases and held it loosely in his hand. He crossed to the closed door the disintegrated woman had been facing and gripped the handle. He turned it—locked.

From behind him, Amos confirmed what was now obvious. "Locked or jammed tight, and so is the other side door outside—we haven't got in there yet and the landlord doesn't have a key. We're waiting on a locksmith. And before you ask, we've already stuck a peep-pipe in and found nothing. So, according to the Preservation of Private Property Act, we gotta sit tight."

Heisen grunted and backed up, looking around the old wooden door, and then reaching up to feel around the frame. From behind, Amos must have been watching.

"Done that—jammed up and no hidden keys. That'd be too easy wouldn't it, Detective Heisen?"

"Yep, sure would." Heisen rolled his eyes and half turned to speak over his shoulder. "Thanks, Amos; I'll take a poke around."

He didn't wait for a reply, instead sliding past the cop and heading for the open door. When he got there, he briefly turned and saw the female agent looking at him. He smiled and winked at her, and she shook her head, but her lips had curved into a small smile.

Still got it, he thought. Outside, he made a sharp turn down a narrow side hallway, continuing on until he came to a door he guessed was the side exit to the room he had just tried to enter. Using the glove again, he jiggled the handle—loose but also jammed. He looked at the frame—this one was more promising; the wood looked old and damp-softened.

Heisen reached inside his jacket, slid free his handgun, and put his ear to the door. Though Amos had said they'd stuck a peep-pipe—a cord camera—into the room, he knew from experience if someone wanted to hide, they could fold themselves into a freakin' suitcase if they took a mind to it.

Heisen let the large gun hang by his side and put his shoulder against the door. He braced one of his legs against the opposite wall in the narrow hallway, and pushed. He gently applied more and more pressure until he felt the wood crunch softly as the lock was torn from its bed in the rotten cavity. He eased the door open and stuck his head inside.

That weird smell again, but stronger—like an electrical short. The word "ozone" immediately leapt into his mind.

He quickly stepped inside but out of the

doorframe's halo of light—nothing like a little backlighting to make you an easy target. He waited for his eyes to adjust to the gloom, and gradually the piles of dirty clothing, food wrappers, and assorted rubbish on a bench-top took on greater definition. The only sound came from the forensics team on the other side of the far door.

Heisen remained motionless and just let his eyes slide around the room. Against the wall was a new pair of jogging shoes, with clean socks tucked into them—incongruously neat amongst the general disarray. On the bench top, a gold chain with a small heart locket, an Yves Saint Laurent wallet open and with several cards in place, a wristwatch—blue Seiko dive model—expensive. *Not theft then*, he thought. *Unless what was taken was something completely different.*

Heisen looked around and grunted. It didn't fit. The entire apartment block was nothing but floor upon floor of piss-smelling flophouses. The picture of the girl, nice, wholesome, the expensive shoes and personal items—it all just didn't damn fit.

Heisen finally walked toward the center of the room as he holstered his gun. *What's wrong with this picture?* He tugged on his lip and he slowly turned in a circle. He hadn't been in the apartment long, but as far as he could tell, the place hadn't been tossed. So, whoever had killed the Sömmer girl had found what they were looking for, or the objective was the girl herself—a hit.

Heisen sighed and put his hands on his hips. Or theory three, it was some sort of freak natural phenomenon—ball lightning, maybe? He snorted softly. That was right up there with it being a microwave killer.

Heisen finally pulled the single glove over his hand. He used a couple of fingers to lift the wallet, carefully sorting through the contents. No receipts, no paperwork, or even a bus ticket…but plenty of cash. *A runner's wallet*, he thought.

He lifted open one of the sleeves and dragged out a picture of the girl. She was with a smiling young man holding an old brown skull. She wore a slightly bored expression and was holding what looked like a weird brushed-metal fountain pen. He turned the photograph over. In small script were five words: *Klaus, me, and his find.* He turned it back over and studied the woman again; at least he now had a clearer image of her face to go with the young woman's name. As well as a lead.

"Klaus, huh? And what did you two kids find?" He studied it for a few more seconds before slipping it into his pocket and quickly checking the wallet's other compartments—all empty.

Heisen sniffed again—ozone. Ozone, and piss, and stale cigarettes, and booze and sex. No Club Med, and definitely not a place you'd expect to find a pretty young girl in new running shoes wearing a thousand Euro Seiko dive watch to be hanging out. From the little information Amos had given him, she'd come here weeks ago and paid her rent cash-in-advance. In places like this, residents came here for hookers, to do drugs deals, or to hide out. You didn't stay for the atmosphere or the local restaurant trade.

He briefly pulled the picture from his pocket and looked again at the smiling face —no way do young girls from good families come here to be incinerated in a two-thousand-degree microburst. Instead, they come here to meet lovers their strict parents didn't approve of...or to hide out. He tapped his chin with a knuckle for a moment. *Yeah, a runner's wallet*, he thought again. *But running from who or what*?

He flicked the light switch but no glow came from the bulb—it was blackened inside. Looking to the door where Amos and his team worked, he saw no key sticking from the lock. On closer inspection, he could see that the locking mechanism was fused —welded shut. He frowned. Whoever came out of this room to freak Doris out and then burn her up, had then come back in here afterward, and then made sure the doors stayed closed.

Heisen looked around; whoever it was had come out of here, come back in here …and had stayed in here. He turned slowly, the Glock hanging loosely at his side.

Where did you go, you sonsofbitches? he thought.

Heisen got down on all fours and looked at floor level under the furniture—there were boxes, dust bunnies, and several cockroaches toes-up amongst the dirt and dust. He got back to his feet and sighed, continuing to turn slowly, trying to think like the person or persons who had been in the room.

He stopped turning; there was only one place left to look. He stepped toward the old closet against the wall and brought the gun up. He laid his hand on the doorknob. An image of the ash outline on the floor flickered in his mind, and he worked to calm his breathing.

One-two-three; he whipped open the door and immediately something leapt at him. He smashed the Glock into it as he fell back and turned side-on, his heart galloping in his chest as he rolled away. He was back on his feet in an instant, gun pointed in a two-handed grip. His vision tunneled as he focused laser-like on the mound lying before him.

"Fuck you too." He exhaled and then laughed softly. "A stupid raincoat." He holstered the gun, relieved he hadn't let off a round. He could imagine the look on Amos' face when the cop busted in to find he had just shot the shit out of a plastic coat.

Heisen lifted his eyes back to the empty closet to continue his investigation. First thing he noticed was that the wooden backboard was blackened. Clothing framed the cupboard rear as if it had already been pushed aside. Heisen reached in and touched the back of the big piece of furniture—it was solid; scorched, but solid. He pushed it—no false wall or sliding panels.

He lifted one of the jackets free and noticed that one side of it was missing. "What the hell?" He brought it closer to his face—it was singed, like the sleeve had been cut away by a red-hot knife. He turned it over in his hands—the other side was untouched. He hung it back up and pulled a shirt from the other side of the cupboard—same thing, but the opposite sleeve—subjected to heat, but no flame—cauterized.

He leant in and looked down at the cupboard floor—no ash. The sleeves and material just...gone. He replaced the shirt and stood back, hands on his hips again. The scorch mark was oval, about three feet high, and he could see now that where the oval and the clothing had overlapped, the sleeves, and other material had simply vanished.

"Hell if I know," he said softly to the dark interior. He pulled off the glove and stuck it in his pocket. He'd run a trace on the girl, and try and find out who the mystery man was. At least now he had names and faces, and somewhere to start.

Heisen paused at the door, looking back at the room. From this angle, the dark oval in the cupboard looked longer, deeper, almost like...a tunnel. He shrugged. *A trick of the eye*, he thought. He gently closed the door behind him. And just in time.

*****

Monroe watched his team move through the rooms like a school of sharks, parting the smaller baitfish as they went. His Defense team didn't work with the police or any other law enforcement body. Those organizations relied on and followed a strict set of regulations and protocols. But who and what his team usually fought didn't obey the rules, so neither did they.

Monroe looked around the room, taking in everything and everyone. His agents, Harper and Felzig, squatted by the outline of the body, taking digital pictures, samples, and readings, and in a few moments, Agent Carter appeared at his side, leaning in close, small box in hand.

"What've you got?" Monroe said.

Carter held up the tiny illuminated screen. "Weird; I've got extremely high gamma radiation traces, bordering on dangerous. Also, several other forms of background trace I can't identify here yet."

Felzig joined them and nodded toward the locked door. "And that room's the focal point."

Monroe turned to the door. "Well, let's have a look then." Monroe crossed the floor.

"Locksmith is on his way," Amos called from behind him.

At the door, Monroe didn't stop, and simply lifted one huge boot and kicked out. The old door exploded inward. He stood in the center of the doorframe, just letting his eyes move over the empty space. Beside him, his agents had already formed up, weapons pointed into the room.

"Clear." He walked in, followed by Benson, Carter holding out his reader, and the huge Raptor with a gun whose laser light probed the dark. They went around the room quickly and professionally. The first sweep was looking for anyone or anything trying to conceal itself. Then they performed a more focused search—looking for trace and clues.

Monroe stood before the open clothes cupboard, looking in at the oval scorch mark. Carter held the reader toward it and half turned.

"Off the scale, right here." He tapped the burn mark with his knuckle. "Solid."

Raptor had appeared beside him. For a big man, he moved silently. "Want me to tell you what I think that looks like?"

Monroe exhaled. "Don't bother, I know." He turned to Carter. "Get those readings back to base. I want to know what those unknown radiation signatures are. And I want them locked in for tracking."

"Yes, sir." Carter began folding his device away.

"Move out." Monroe turned away. "We've already missed this party. Let's try and get in front of the next one."

At the door, he stopped and gave Amos a

small salute. "Thank you for your cooperation, officer."

"Like I had any choice." The old cop snorted as Monroe left the room

CHAPTER 09

BERLIN – KRIMINALPOLIZERI HEADQUARTERS

Detective Ed Heisen sat down heavily, switched on his computer, and pulled the holo-frame toward him, also switching it on.

He reached into his pocket for the picture of Doris and Klaus. Though he had faces and first names, he also had a surname for the deceased. Although at this stage, given the state of the body, no prints, teeth, identifying marks, and as there was very little forensic evidence to point to it even being a woman, he would have to just assume it was Doris for now.

He stuck the picture in the holo projector, and an image appeared on his desk. The software cleaned it up, making best guesses at indistinct areas, and Heisen studied the two young people—both good looking, healthy and fit, and probably late 20s, maybe he was 30, give or take.

He began to run a search on the woman and quickly found that she was born in Wolfsburg in the state of lower Saxony. Heisen whistled. It was a rich city, and in fact, the richest in Germany.

He dug some more and found that Wolfsburg was both the 5th largest city in Germany and the majority of its inhabitants worked in the Volkswagen headquarters and car plant located here, which was the largest in the world.

"Still money in cars," he said and did a little more searching.

Sure enough, he found that Doris' father, Hans Gunter Sömmer, was a VP at the Volkswagen headquarters. He drilled down on their address, and the huge estate was brought up on his screen.

He whistled and sat back with his arms folded for a moment. "Got any enemies, Dad?"

It also confirmed his assumption that she was hiding out. This girl did not need to stay in some lower town flophouse because she wanted or needed to.

But if he wanted to find out exactly why, it would have to be from the guy she had been there with—if he was still alive.

"So, who are you, dear Klaus?"

Heisen then tried looking for any known associates of Doris' named Klaus—he checked her old jobs, high school and college student enrollments, and even tried a few aliases, but nothing showed up.

"Great, he's the invisible fucking man."

The phone on his desk rang, making him jump, and he sprung forward to grab it. "Detective Heisen."

He listened for a moment. "Good man, hold on…" he reached for a pad and pen. "…go on."

Heisen wrote down the results of the tests on the ash, and after a few moments shook his aching hand. "Slow down, slow down." He exhaled through his nose and made more rapid notes as he tried to keep up with the information flow.

"Thanks, Jerry, I owe you a beer." He grinned. "Okay, two beers." He hung up and held the notes up.

The organic matter was fully incinerated to a point where there was no DNA or any trace of identifying biological markers. He sighed and read on.

To obtain that level of total carbonization, significant heat was generated. At a minimum, it was expected to have been 2,000 degrees

Fahrenheit.

"Tell me something I don't know, buddy."

Jerry had included some heat sources as examples: An industrial furnace burned at 750 degrees; a toxic waste disposal unit achieved temperatures of 1,500 degrees to ensure even the residue gases were destroyed. However, an oxyacetylene torch, that combined oxygen and gas to create a pinpoint blue flame, could reach a contact heat of 5,400 degrees.

In regard to the torch, Jerry had made some additional comments on this one—to render a body to ash, including the heavier bones, it would need to be subject to all-over application of the torch flame for approximately 6 hours.

"Bullshit."

Heisen threw the notes onto his desk and leaned far back in his chair to rub both hands up through his hair. Bottom line, there was nothing that could have generated that sort of focused heat, in such a short period of time, without it being the size of a truck, or destroying everything else in that apartment.

After another moment, he sprung forward. "Time to earn my pay." He stood, grabbed the picture from the holo-frame, and headed for the door.

CHAPTER 10

NEW BERLIN, GERMANIA – COMMAND

The general's voice boomed inside the large room. Senior science officers and Cleanup team leaders sat looking down at hands clasped on the desk. All except Jax.

"Every zone trip costs us close to a trillion glots." He looked from Gilbred to Jax. "And both of you are now into me for about ten times that much."

The general walked slowly along behind the rows of seats and sighed. "This is turning out to be a real shit day." He continued for another few feet and stopped behind Gilbred, who obviously sensed the big man and visibly gulped.

The general leaned around in front of the science officer. "Gilbred, isn't it?" The general grinned like a shark and didn't wait for the man to respond. "You and your entire science division better start pinpointing better zones for us right now. Because, if we keep stepping in and out of that sort of zone, sooner or later something bad is going to happen."

The general's jaws worked. "Because in that zone, they're getting smarter, and I for one don't want to be around when one of those big ugly mothers works out how to follow us back up the pipe to here." He straightened but kept one large hand on the back of the man's neck. "So, just to be clear. I couldn't give a fuck about you, your division, or anyone else in this goddamn room."

The general pushed off from Gilbred and turned to face Jax. "Soldier, take a proximity bomb—if you can't get your hands on the burner, then get as close as you can and take every-fucking-thing out nearby. I authorize you to use all force necessary to retrieve or destroy the device. There will not be a time-quake on my watch."

"Sir, yes sir." Jax sat straighter. "Permission to take language converters and conduct Monst interrogations, sir."

The general turned. "Authorized, Master Cleaner." He folded his arms and glared at Gilbred. "Get it done, and get it done quickly. No traces, no evidence. Retrieval or destruction—no other options."

Jax stood and half bowed. "Retrieval or destruction, sir, yes sir."

The Master Cleaner headed for the door with a smile on his lips—Monst interrogation fully authorized. *That's more like it*, he thought.

CHAPTER 11

PALEONTOLOGY DEPT, UNIVERSITY OF
TÜBINGEN, BADEN-WÜRTTEMBERG

Professor Julius Cohen, the head of paleontology, hummed as he collected his morning mail and headed to the staff room. He was early and first in as always, so he put the coffee on. The tradeoff was he got the room to himself for at least the first hour of the day.

The solitude and silence was a worthy payment before the roar of students filled the halls, plus the inane chatter of his colleagues.

He let the envelopes of varying sizes and a few packages spill from under his arm onto a desk, and went to fill the coffee machine. The new machine was blisteringly fast, and as he never added cream, he could start drinking in just a few minutes.

Once done, Cohen sat down and sorted the mail into various piles—the first was for bills and brochures. He'd deal with that last. The second was for names and places he recognized. That would be next. And then there was the urgent, or the interesting, that got dealt with as a priority. After all, that was usually the fun stuff.

His eyes immediately found the brown paper-covered box. It had some weight to it, and he gave it a small shake, feeling something move inside. He didn't recognize the name on top, but as the shipping tag indicated an archeological specimen, his interest was immediately piqued.

He pulled a small penknife from his pocket and carefully cut through the string, then tore the paper free. Next he cut through the tape and opened the box.

Sorting in amongst the wadded newspaper, he found the hard object and lifted it out. Cohen smiled as he looked down at the piece.

"Well, well, well."

He lifted it in one hand and turned it slowly. "Lower mandible, possibly, probably, *Homo Neanderthalensis*…and very beautiful."

He suddenly wished he was wearing gloves. Cohen brought the fossil closer to his face and sniffed, smelling the earthy fragrance of time, aged mustiness, and a composition of various minerals.

The paleontology professor stood up so he was nearer to the overhead lights and examined it up close. There were still some fragments of rocky matrix sticking to the bone, so it had been excavated quite recently, and he could tell it was done by an amateur.

It needed professional cleaning; however, it was still a magnificent piece. *But who sent it? Why? And where was the rest?* he wondered. He had so many questions.

"Fascinating." He held the small brown jawbone in one hand and reached for the box to read off the name again.

The soft sound behind him would normally have irritated him a little as it meant his colleagues had arrived to share the staff room. But today, he was keen to show off his new prize.

Cohen turned. "Looks like I've got a fan…"

He froze. And then blinked several times as if to clear his vision. No words could come as he simply stared with an open mouth.

The light that engulfed him tingled for less than a second. After that there was nothing as Professor Julius Cohen, the box, and the bone sample, all ceased to exist.

CHAPTER 12

BERLIN – WELFARE DISTRICT

Klaus Hoffman scribbled the note as quickly as he could, folded it once, and then dropped it into the box on top of the fossil. Picking up the tape gun, he set about sealing it, then writing a name and address on the top. He finished by plastering it with way too many stamps.

He closed his eyes for a moment to try and calm himself as his racing heartbeat was making him feel slightly nauseous. He opened his eyes and held up the package, looking again at the name he'd written. The only teacher he had ever listened to—the American professor, Matt Kearns. When it came to all things old or all things weird, Kearns seemed to know everything about everything.

"And no charge for this one, Professor." He

giggled with just a hint of panicked insanity. "My last good deed."

Klaus looked at his watch—half-past four—he had to get back to Doris and check in before it got dark. She'd panic if she didn't hear from him by nightfall. It was his idea that they split up, as he bet they were looking for a couple. At least this way he could move quickly if he needed to.

He jumped to his feet and walked to the door, placed his ear against it to listen for a second, and then quickly unlocked the multiple bolts. Klaus opened it just an inch and looked through the crack. He planned to run to the mail chute at the end of the hallway, throw in the package, and then be back inside in under fifteen seconds.

Just as he was about to dart out, a door at the other end of the corridor opened and old Mrs. Silberman started easing herself out—tent-like, stained cotton dress, and wiry gray hair that he remembered once had a small piece of toast crust stuck in it.

Klaus cursed, shut his door, and leaned back against it, surprised at how his heart rate had jumped up again for nothing.

"Calm down, calm down. Next thing *you'll* be the one seeing goblins," he whispered to himself.

"*Goblins.*"

He laughed again as he let his eyes slide around the small decrepit room. The place was a mess, but it didn't matter; he and Doris would move again by the end of the week. It only took Doris a few days before she said she felt like she was being watched. It was always the same—there was whispering going on in the walls and she was sure her place was bugged.

Klaus sighed; he loved her but she was driving him crazy and becoming more paranoid by the day—and making *him* more paranoid by the day. *Lunacy was infectious*, he guessed.

The final straw was when she told him she thought she saw a little goblin watching her...a freaking goblin for Chrissake.

He looked at his room again—all the windows were taped over with newspaper, the phone had been pulled from the wall, all the power sockets taped over, and even the door keyholes blocked up.

"Yeah, she's paranoid, but I'm fine." He laughed out loud this time.

His one luxury was the ancient television that remained on day and night. He looked across to the old cathode ray-style box as the robotic newsreader reeled off the names of the latest drive-by shooting victims, domestic violence punching bags, and other assorted attacks on the human herd of life.

But the next story about a bizarre murder was like an ice pick to the back of the neck—Professor Julius Cohen, the head of paleontology at the University of Tübingen, was believed the victim of a bizarre execution. His remains were as yet formally unidentified, and it was expected that confirmation might not be possible given the state of the body.

Klaus walked toward the television, the package still under his arm, and stood trance-like before the flickering screen. The final part of the story nearly made him double over. Cohen's apparent murder brought the number of bizarre killings to three, as Julius Cohen now joined Professors Carl Ingram and Rudi Hokstetor as victims in what police were dubbing the Incinerator Murders.

Klaus' mouth hung open. *Cohen, Ingram, and Hokstetor*—he knew those men, knew *all* of them. Because he had sent each and every one of them a piece of the fossil skeleton.

He flopped back into a ratty armchair and grabbed his head. Did he do that? Was it his fault they were dead? Was someone killing anyone who touched the bones? He knew that the complete skeleton was valuable but he didn't think it was worth killing people for.

He carefully put the box down on the tabletop and backed away from it.

"Think, think." He paced quickly around the small room. "Gotta get out." He started filling his pockets with his wallet, phone, and keys when a knock on the door made him cry out. He quickly put a hand over his mouth and listened.

The knock came again. "Klaus? Hello, Klaus, are you there? My Timmy-Tims has got out of his cage again and I need your help. Klaus?"

Oh for fuck's sake, he exhaled. Old Mrs. Silberman and that parakeet would be the death of him. Do one good deed and suddenly you're an adopted son…and one required to do everything from change light bulbs to recapturing bad-tempered parrots that had more escape routines up their feathered asses than freaking Houdini. Plus a beak sharp enough to slice bacon.

Klaus stayed where he was, thinking through his options. Should he scream at her to fuckoff? That'd send a clear message. He grimaced; *nah*, much as he'd love for her to leave him alone, he wasn't quite ready to be a total asshole just yet.

He eased himself down in the chair. He'd wait her out. The knocking continued. He looked at his watch again and rubbed his head, glaring at the door.

C'mon, Mrs. Silberman, go home, willya? He needed to get the fuck outta here and find Doris. His eyes slid to the walls; he suddenly had a bad feeling about this place.

CHAPTER 13

THE DEFENSE BUNKER

Monroe stood staring at the map on the wall. There were red pins in it and he tried to make sense of their placement.

"Any patterns?" Carter asked.

After a moment, Monroe exhaled through his nose and slowly shook his head. "Looks random to me but probably isn't." He placed his hands on his hips. "They're searching for something. They know what it is, and sort of where to look, but they keep striking out so they're still looking, is my guess."

"So, you think it's definitely an intrusion?" Raptor asked from over their shoulders.

"No proof of that," Monroe said, but half turned. "But gut feel? Yeah, I do. Something has been paying us a visit. And leaving a damn mess behind every time."

"Time to fuck 'em up," Raptor said. "Pay back."

"Yeah, but we gotta find them first." Monroe turned. "We need more eyes and ears. Might be worthwhile being nice to the cops. They don't know what they're looking for, but they seem to be getting to the hot zones first."

"Make 'em work for us." Carter grinned.

Monroe shrugged. "They're servants of the public after all, right?"

CHAPTER 14

BERLIN – KRIMINALPOLIZERI HEADQUARTERS

Heisen flopped back into his chair, exhausted. He spent the previous day combing the city and hadn't found any clue to where this mysterious Klaus was hiding out.

He bet his last credit that the guy was in some other doss house, but given there were millions of them, he needed a tip-off, some luck, or a better functioning brain.

He sighed and read through his notes again. In the following days, more bodies had turned up—or better said, more bodies had burned up. The coroner had hinted at spontaneous combustion—also alcohol abuse, ball lightning, faulty wiring, all were listed as possible causes. But none of the suggestions actually explained the amount of heat generated, the peculiar explicit targeting of individuals, nor the ability of the heat source to simply switch on and off.

Funny thing was, Heisen was beginning to see a pattern. The closer he came to finding this Klaus guy, the more the ash trails began to pile up. Coincidence, or was there a link?

Out of needing luck, more brainpower, or a tip-off, it was the last one that came in first; he recognized the whispered voice over the phone—a young cop he'd helped out once before. The guy informed him that something was going down in the down-and-out quarter of town. Sergeant Amos had been assigned and was en route, which meant it was probably related to his case.

"I owe you one," he said, hung up, and went out the door so quick he felt like he was flying.

Twenty minutes later, Heisen bounded up the stairs, knocking once on the open door, holding up his badge and heading straight over to where Amos talked with some other uniforms.

"Officer Amos; another nice day for a cookout?" Heisen raised an eyebrow and grinned. But the older cop half turned, gave him a look like he'd just noticed dog shit on his shoe, and immediately went back to talking softly with his younger colleagues. Heisen waited, scanning the apartment, trying to take everything in.

Finally, Amos issued last instructions to his men and turned to him. "Cookout? You must be the brains of the Kripo, *huh*?" Amos said as he sauntered away.

Heisen followed. "Hey, lighten up, will ya? I just—"

Amos spun at him, stepping in closer. "You just what? Listen, Heisen, why don't you shut the hell up, unless you've got some answers for us? You know, from all your de-tect-ing work. Because we got corpses piling up..." he snorted, "...what's left of 'em, and we got zip, zero, nada."

Ed Heisen frowned, taken back by the animosity in the normally laconic police sergeant. The guy must have been getting his ass seriously kicked by his boss. He held up his hands. "Okay, sorry." Heisen motioned to the forensics guys moving about in the next room. "What have you got: another carbonized corpse?"

"Yes and no." Amos' lips then compressed as he led the detective into the kitchen. Heisen smelled the odor that was becoming too familiar to him—ozone. Amos pointed to the thing in the corner.

Heisen winced. "Christ."

The body, or partial body, was laid out on the floor—the arms and legs were nothing but ash outlines, to the shoulders and hips, where the body was intact again. The head was still attached, but gruesomely, one eye, the ears, and the nose were gone—seared away, but black and cauterized. As usual, there was no sign of blood, as if something had snap-burnt the limbs and facial features away.

"Well?" Amos went down on his haunches and swept his hand over the remains. "C'mon, Detective, tell me what you think?"

Heisen crouched beside Amos to study the woman, or what was left of her. Mid-seventies, cheap cotton dress in need of a clean, nothing of value on her. Her hair was wiry and gray, and looked like it also needed a wash. But it was her face that drew his attention—even though one eye, the nose, and ears had been removed, he could see the mix of pain and fear still imprinted in the twist of the remaining features.

"Torture."

"Jesus Christ!" Amos jumped as the word floated in from behind them. Heisen spun to see the tall black-clad agent standing right behind him and towering over them.

The agent's eyes moved over the old woman's body. He squatted beside Amos; not apologizing

85

for startling the old cop. Heisen noticed that even crouching he was a head taller. Amos swallowed and turned back to the crime scene.

"Who are you?" asked Heisen, not expecting an answer.

"Call me Monroe," said the big man. He clasped his hands together on his knees. "In the Congo, we lost a man on a mission. When we finally found him and recovered his body, his bones had been broken, starting at the fingers and toes, the impact trauma moving slowly up to his hips and shoulders. Would have taken hours, and been agony."

Someone else squatted on the other side of him, and he turned to see the female agent, Felzig, he thought he heard her being called, and she nudged Heisen's arm.

"Bad shit, huh?"

"That it is." He continued to look at her. The woman was probably early thirties and had short hair cut in a boyish style. Her chin was square and had a scar down one side of it. But her eyes were a luminous blue that crinkled with humor. He liked that.

"I think your boss is right." He nodded toward the corpse. "I've seen that sort of torture before as well—on the poor saps the Columbian drug gangs had their fun with. Pretty vicious stuff."

"Yep…especially brutal to use on an old lady." She held out a hand. "Felzig, *Greta*."

"Greta." He gripped her hand and held it. "Heisen, Ed, senior detective with the Kripo. And who are you with?"

She stood, holding his hand and taking him with her. "With him." She nodded at the crouching Monroe.

Heisen looked across at the big man who turned to him and nodded. "Detective Heisen."

Monroe then turned to the obliterated old woman and continued to study her remains. He put a finger in the ash and first rubbed his fingers together, feeling the texture, and then brought it to his nose and sniffed. He slowly rose to his feet and yelled over his shoulder.

"Carter, got a partial body in here."

Heisen grimaced down at the remains. "So, you really think she was tortured?"

"Wait a minute." Amos frowned and leaned around in front of them. "You were serious?" He pointed at the partial corpse. "Agnes Silberman, seventy-seven, with arthritis in both hips and chronic diabetes. She's on the pension and lives with a freaking parrot. Why the fuck would someone want to torture her?" His voice rose.

"What the hell has this old lady got that someone would do that to her for?"

Heisen looked back at the dry scabbing on the wounds. "What has she got? Maybe not money, maybe nothing…or maybe all she had was information. Something in her head."

"Nothing opens memory's doors like a little pain," Monroe said.

"A little?" Heisen scoffed as he looked again at how the old woman's arms and legs had been burned all the way to her torso.

Another agent, Heisen assumed it was Carter, entered with a box case and immediately set to work sampling the air, examining the body, and even slicing away some of her skin at her arm's cauterization line. He pulled out a probe and lifted an edge of her dress. He let it drop and then examined the ground beside her, leaning in close to a small outline pressed into one of the ash pipes that used to be a leg.

He turned to Monroe. "Got an impression." He reached into his bag, pulled out a small can, shook it, and then sprayed something that fell lightly onto the small indentation and then foamed up. After a second, it changed color and settled flat. Carter carefully lifted it out and dusted off the excess ash. He stood and held it out to Monroe.

Amos and Heisen tried to see around the big man. Monroe looked at it, his eyes narrowing. He waved it away. "Bag it."

Amos squinted at the object as Carter placed it into a small clear envelope. "Is that supposed to be a footprint?"

Heisen nodded. "Looks like one...if you're about two feet tall."

"Kid maybe?" Amos responded, his eyes following the bag as Carter took it back to the case he'd brought in with him.

Heisen shrugged. "Sure it is, and why not? Some kid with a laser. You can get all kinda shit online these days."

Monroe snorted and turned away. Heisen edged in closer to Felzig.

"You ever seen this sort of thing before?"

Her mouth turned down momentarily. "I've seen some bad stuff and some weird stuff over the years. But never seen anything like this. It's a new one." She turned. "You?"

"Same, about seeing some oddities, but not this high temperature and focused incineration. I can't even work out how it might have been done."

She nodded.

"Greta, wasn't it?" He smiled again.

She tilted her head toward him. "And Fred,

right?"

He shrugged. "Ed, so close enough."

She chuckled. "You're all right, *Ed*."

"I do my best." He quickly looked over his shoulder at her colleagues. "If you ever feel like unwinding, and going for a drink or something…"

She raised an eyebrow. "You get many dates at crime scenes?"

He shrugged. "Sure. It's where the coolest people hang out."

She chuckled. "No need to try so hard, Ed." Felzig reached up to put a hand on the back of his neck and squeezed lightly. "Okay, sure, why not. Be seeing you, Detective."

"I'll get your number, next…" He watched her go.

"*Boss*," was said from outside the room.

Monroe's head whipped around at the sound of the voice. "Yo." He turned back briefly to Carter. "Finish up," Monroe said as he left the room.

Ed Heisen looked back at the woman's ruined body for a moment before turning back to Carter. The man was down low, waving a small box around. He pointed it at Mrs. Silberman's corpse. Heisen knelt beside him.

"Weird shit," Heisen said.

Carter grunted, keeping his eyes on the small box. Heisen looked over his shoulder and decided to try his luck. He nodded toward the instrument. "Pretty unusual readings."

Carter grunted again, staying focused on the small illuminated screen. "Got that right. At least we identified it—Xenon."

"Xenon? I've heard of that; isn't it the weird stuff used in things like flash lamps?" Heisen looked back at Mrs. Silberman.

Carter shook his head. "Not this type. This is 135. Normally, Xenon is a gas that occurs in the Earth's atmosphere, consists of about eight stable isotopes, and five times that many unstable ones— pretty normal stuff. But 135 is different; it's not naturally occurring. Used as the propellant for ion thrusters in spacecraft, it's also a neutron absorber in reactors and is usually the result of nuclear fission. So nope, free-range Xenon-135 should not be here at all."

Heisen whistled as he stood. "Like I said; weird shit."

Heisen turned to Amos, grabbed him by the arm, and led him out of the room. "Hey, have you looked in the other apartments yet?"

Amos shook his head. "Next thing on the list."

"Good." Heisen let him go. "One more thing;

anything else weird in here?"

Amos frowned, and then his brows unlocked and he thumbed over his shoulder. Heisen followed where he indicated and saw a birdcage that had a few charred feathers inside.

"Oh shit, not the parrot as well. Those monsters." Heisen suppressed a grin and tried again. "Anything else? Burn marks in odd places maybe?"

"Oh yeah, in the bathroom. Looks like the old girl set fire to something—big black oval on the wall." Amos' eyes narrowed. "How'd you know about that?"

Heisen pointed at his head. "Good ole *de-tecting* work."

*****

Monroe stood with Felzig in the bathroom. There was a three-foot black scorch mark on the wall under the sink. Felzig turned and raised her eyebrows, holding out the small reader in her hands.

Monroe exhaled. "Let me guess, gamma off the scale, and more traces of Xenon-135?"

She nodded. Carter and Benson joined them, and Monroe turned to Carter. "What could have done that?"

Carter shook his head. "We've got HEL tech mounted on our destroyers. Those High Energy Lasers work at around a hundred kilowatts—that'd do it. Also some industrial lasers, but they're not portable." He shrugged. "Bottom line: nothing we've got." He looked up. "And we got the most advanced in the world."

"In *our* world." Monroe stared back out into the hallway. "Someone or something is coming in and out, with some pretty high-grade tech...and given what they did to the old woman, seems they're here to play hardball."

Monroe turned away. "We can do that too."

*****

In the apartment down the hall, Heisen went quickly from room to room, stopping at one littered with packing tape and brown paper. On the debris-strewn table sat an unsent package. He spun it around and read the label—Professor Matt Kearns.

He thought about it for just 3 seconds. "Fuck it." He ripped it open.

"Alas, poor Yorick." Heisen lifted out the skull, holding the brown relic up in his hands. He smiled. "Nice to finally meet you, the elusive Mr. Klaus."

Heisen put the skull down and dug deeper into the package, finding an envelope addressed to the American professor. He tore it open and quickly scanned through it. There was a brief introduction from Klaus, and then a description of his find—a complete Neanderthal skeleton, plus one other item. Heisen frowned, remembering the picture of Doris Sömmer holding the small metallic device.

"One other item, *hmm*? His 'find' maybe?"

He ripped the guy's name from the package and stuck it in his pocket. Then he totally emptied the box on the table, but there was nothing else inside.

"So where is it?"

He turned slowly in the small room. There was a dark scar on the far wall. The curtains hanging beside it had been seared away in a perfect facsimile of the oval burn. Heisen looked back at the letter in his hands. It was signed 'K' and had a single mobile phone number at the bottom.

He pulled out his phone and dialed. It answered after the first ring. He smiled.

"Hello, Klaus."

CHAPTER 15

BERLIN – GROSSER TIERGARTEN PARK

It took Heisen most of the day and a dozen more calls to convince the young man he was who he said he was. But eventually Klaus relented, and…spoke.

The kid sounded at near panic stage, and unfortunately Heisen was the one to have to break the bad news on Doris—big mistake, and he suddenly felt he should have avoided being so honest. Klaus went from panic to raging madness, and Heisen knew he was close to disappearing for good. It took the detective another 20 minutes to convince Klaus that he was the kid's only option he had left if he wanted to stay alive.

Heisen now sat on a park bench, desperately

wanting to meet with him and waiting for his phone to ring. He looked up at the sky, watching the clouds lengthen and fragment, and he turned his focus inward, sorting through what he knew in his mind. Klaus and Doris had found something in Germany—a fossil Neanderthal skeleton and something else, as yet undetermined.

It seemed people who had been associated with the young pair were getting themselves killed, and unpleasantly. Heisen felt his curiosity was becoming unbearable —he was determined to solve the crimes, but more than that he just damn wanted to know what the hell was going on.

The kid wouldn't give him any details over the phone, but confirmed they found something strange entombed with the fossil—something that didn't belong there.

Now, the girl was dead, many of the scientists that Klaus had sent bits of the skeleton to were dead, and his landlady was dead...and added to that, she died after being tortured, horribly. It was a trail a mile wide, and leading straight to Mr. Klaus Hoffman.

If the group of people had just been hit over the head or stabbed or maybe even shot, Heisen might conclude they were only after the skeleton. A find that one museum expert had suggested to him, if it was intact, could be worth half a million. Big money, especially considering you could get someone whacked for a measly fifty Euros these days.

But the way the murders were executed defied belief—burned down to dust, and nobody had any idea what type of device or weapon was used— even one from the military's research and development arsenals. And the kicker was the throwaway comment by the coroner: "*out of this world,*" she had said, as she closed the book on the Sömmer girl's inquest.

"Out of this world," Heisen repeated softly.

The detective turned his head and caught a glimpse of a familiar head of blond hair in the passenger seat of a car that was stopped at lights. He shot to his feet.

"Johanna?"

Heisen took a few steps, lifting his phone and starting to dial her number, even though he promised himself he wouldn't.

Hey, look to the left. Guess who? He was going to say with a smile in his voice. But then she sat back in her seat, and he saw the man beside her.

She laughed as he obviously said something amusing to her. Heisen stopped dialing and dropped his arm. The guy in the car was younger than he was, fitter, and just looked…better. Most depressing thing of all was she looked really happy.

Anger quickly morphed to understanding, and then to resignation. He only had himself to blame, he guessed. Heisen turned and walked slowly back to his park bench and dropped heavily onto it.

"Greta Felzig seemed interested…a little."

He jumped when the phone rang in his hand. "Shit." He quickly jammed it against his ear. "Detective Edward Heisen."

There was a pause, and then: "It's me."

For some insane reason, he thought it was going to be Johanna, but then he breathed a sigh of relief at hearing the young man's fear-filled voice.

"Hi, Klaus. How you doing?"

Several seconds of silence greeted his question, and Heisen thought he would ring off. But there came an intake of breath, a clearing of the throat, and then Klaus came back on.

"Not good."

"We can help you," Heisen responded automatically.

"Bullshit. No one can. There's fucking little people after me…and they can walk right through the walls."

Heisen squeezed the phone as he concentrated. "What do you mean by little people?"

"I'm not mad," Klaus said softly.

"I know you're not. In fact, I believe you, because I've seen one of their footprints."

"You have? You know they're real?" His voice became shrill.

"Like I said, I believe you. Tell me where you are, son." Heisen felt he was holding his breath.

The silence stretched again. "Wilson Street...number 17. Third floor, apartment 3B. It's an old brownstone."

Heisen knew the area and told him so. "It'll take me 20 minutes to get to you. Stay inside and keep the doors locked."

"Are you shitting me? I'm never going outside again." Klaus rung off.

CHAPTER 16

THE DEFENSE BUNKER

"Yo, he's found him." Greta Felzig took the small communication plug from her ear. "I knew planting that bug on him would pay off."

"That's our boy." Monroe got to his feet. "Where is he?"

"17 Wilson Street, apartment 3B." She turned and smiled. "Heisen hasn't called it in, so he's going in alone."

Monroe checked his watch. "He'll get there first." He stared off into the distance for a moment before coming to a decision. "Let's armor up…just in case our little friends decide to make an appearance."

Raptor appeared in the doorway. "About time. Let's go stomp some tiny people ass."

CHAPTER 17

BERLIN – NORTHERN NEUKÖLLN

Heisen pulled in to the curb and sat for a moment as he examined the dark brown building on Wilson Street. He briefly looked over his shoulder and down the empty, wet street—it wasn't a great area and he just hoped his car was waiting for him when he returned.

Heisen craned forward in his seat to look back up at the building's dark and anonymous edifice. *Klaus still staying underground*, he thought.

"Little people," he said to the windscreen as he searched for anything out of the ordinary in the building's third-floor windows. "Goddamn little people."

If he'd had the conversation in an Irish bar, he would have got the joke. But the weird oval burn holes, the even weirder way people were being killed, and the tiny footprints left behind in Mrs. Silberman's ash outline—those tiny, perfect, military-style boot prints—he didn't think it was a kid for a second. The foot was too narrow—like an adult's, but smaller. Something was seriously weird and it was no joke.

"Little people," he said again softly and then snorted. "Little people, walking through walls, with laser guns, torturing our citizens." He laughed out loud. "Haven't had a drop to drink, Chief, honest."

He checked his gun and pushed out of the car to stand looking up at the brownstone. It was a formidable, old-style building with small windows, and so much dour brickwork it looked like it was constructed from coffee grounds and dark chocolate.

He counted up three floors—somewhere up there, his rendezvous waited. He noticed all the windows were shut and drapes pulled tight.

"Please be alive, Klaus." He headed up to the small landing, pushed open the large double doors, and then sprang lightly up the several flights of stairs to the third floor.

As Heisen approached 3B, he slowed, walking lightly now. At the door, he leaned forward to listen for a second or two but heard nothing. He knocked once and immediately stood to the side— old habits die hard, especially after you've seen half a dozen hollow-nose slugs tear through a door dead center in response to the old, *open up, it's the police*, request.

Heisen waited. There was movement inside.

"Who is it?" whispered from behind the door.

Heisen stayed with his back against the wall. "Detective Heisen, Klaus. Lemme in."

"How do I know it's you?" Klaus' voice was high and tight with fear.

Heisen groaned and resisted the urge to swear, deciding instead to cut the kid some slack given he still sounded scared shitless. "Klaus, we just spoke 20 minutes ago…" He lowered his voice, "…about the little people."

A bolt slid back, and then what sounded like packing tape being ripped from around the frame. The door opened a crack, the security chain still hanging in place. The eye ran him up and down, and the door closed for a second, to be immediately pulled back open.

Heisen guessed he looked enough like a cop to pass the test. He stepped inside. A pale youth stood in the muted darkness wearing a stained T-shirt, jeans, and bare feet. His eyes looked sunken—he guessed the kid needed some hot food and about a week's worth of sleep.

Heisen quickly looked him over for weapons—old habits again. He sniffed; the place stunk of body odor, cigarettes, and mildew.

Klaus half smiled. "It's not much, but it's home."

Heisen smiled back and nodded, letting the kid unwind.

Klaus motioned to a Formica table and chairs. "I'd offer you a drink, but there's nothing left. I ran out of food a few days back and have been too scared to go out." His eyes narrowed. "*Uh*, do you have anything? Food I mean."

Heisen shook his head. "Just some gum."

Klaus seemed to think about it for a few seconds, and then shrugged. "Okay." He held out his hand.

Heisen gave him the pack and Klaus jammed a few sticks into his mouth, chewed for a few seconds, and then swallowed the entire mass. He quickly stuffed the rest in and did the same.

Heisen sat down. "So, tell me about the little people?"

Klaus swallowed again, breathing heavily and savoring his first meal in days. He sat down heavily and looked up with exhausted eyes.

"They're after me."

"You said that," Heisen said. "What do you think they want?"

"They want what I found," Klaus responded lethargically.

Heisen shrugged. "The fossil—the Neanderthal skeleton—that?"

"No, no, I don't think so. I mean, I did at first, but not anymore. It was what the caveman had in his hand." He rummaged around in his pocket. "This...they want me because of *this*." He placed his fist on the table, and then opened his hand.

Heisen leaned forward. It looked like a fat fountain pen, brushed chrome and about three inches long with a slight bulge at one end. He squinted. There seemed to be a glow coming from inside.

"It's still working." Heisen sat back.

Klaus licked his lips. "I know, and that's impossible. The matrix we dug the fossil from was at least fifty thousand years old. Whoever, or whatever, dropped this thing was around at the time Neanderthals were spearing mammoths on the German steppes." His mouth worked for a second or two before finally finding the words. "I don't think it came from our world."

Heisen frowned as he stared at the object.

"And now they want it back."

Klaus nodded. "Maybe it was invisible to them when it was buried, but soon as we dug it out, the shit started happening. I've got to get rid of it. You take it." Klaus slid it across the table.

Heisen didn't move to touch it, and Klaus just made a noise in his throat and rubbed his face so hard, the skin actually moved up and down like a sagging mask.

Heisen squinted at it. "What does it do?"

Klaus took his hands from his face and now looked about 80 years old. "I don't know, and I don't fucking care. I just want to get rid of the damned thing." He lunged at Heisen. "I know… I know what it is…it's a goddamn homing device or something like that. That's why they keep finding me."

He stood so quickly his chair flipped back onto the floor. "I just need to give it back and get on with my life." He paced, wringing his hands. "But these little things came out of the wall—just walked right out of it. I held it out to them, but they freaked. I bolted and ran into Mrs. Silberman's apartment. But they came in after me. I… I jumped out her window and ran, and kept running."

He snatched the thing up in his hand and

shook his head, his eyes crushed shut. "Is she okay? Mrs. Silberman, I mean. I tried calling her, but a cop answered."

Heisen continued to watch the young man. Following his reaction to Doris being killed, he had no urge to tell him he got the old lady tortured and burned up.

"Klaus, we'll get you to a safe house. Get someone to have a look at that device and find out exactly what it is. Maybe work out why they want it so bad."

Klaus scoffed. "A safe house? There's no such thing with these guys. Have you not been listening to me? These little freaks walk through walls. I'd last about…"

"We'll have you guarded twenty-four-seven. I give you my word." Heisen shrugged. "Besides, once it's out of your possession, they'll probably lose interest, right?"

"No, it doesn't matter now. I've touched it, so they'll find me." Klaus looked up. "I'm probably cursed."

Heisen waited a few seconds. He could see the young man's mind was ticking over. He looked again at his emaciated frame. "One thing's for sure: you can't keep going like this; you'll be dead from starvation in a week."

Klaus dropped his head into his hands and rubbed the fingers hard through his shockwave of dusty hair. "Maybe I'd be better off dead." He sighed and sat back, his eyes and cheeks sunken like a shipwreck survivor.

Heisen noticed Klaus' lips were so dry they were flaking. He got to his feet. "Stay here, kid. I'll get you some water. Then I'll call in some backup and we can get you safely out of here." He smiled down at the cowering youth. "First thing though, I want a doc to look at you, okay?"

Klaus nodded, resting his head back in his hands. The device remained on the table, glowing softly. Klaus stared at it as though in a trance.

Heisen thought it seemed to pulse now, like a small heartbeat. One thing was for sure: he didn't want to pick it up either.

CHAPTER 18

NEW BERLIN, PORTAL ROOM – FINAL JUMP

"We got a big pulse. Good, strong signature." The portal controller's hands flew over the command console. "Tracking, tracking—*got it*—verified trace."

He leaned back in his chair toward Jax, who stood with brow lowered and arms folded.

"Time and position identified—excellent proximity confirmation, sir." He smiled at the brutal soldier. "I can put you within three feet of our missing burner."

Jax's chest swelled and he turned to roar to his team. "Muscle up, people. This is the big one."

He and his crew had been on standby, all ready and fully kitted out for hours now. Jax had pulled together a big team, and this time they were bringing back that burner; there was no other option.

Jax was under no illusion what could be waiting for them—this time zone meant Monst with a few atoms of brainpower, and that moved the lethality up the scale. He also knew that his Cleaners had made so much noise in that zone that they would have been noticed by now—and that spelled trouble.

But as far as he was concerned, the general had given him all the authority he needed to get the job done. And if he had to burn the entire building to the ground, and every fucking Monst in it, then so be it.

His team lined up, two-abreast, all in their nano-body armor over iron-hard muscles. Some had painted skulls or other images of dealing death on their armor; Jax liked it. He walked along their line, seeing the gritty determination in their eyes and set of their chins.

"This day, we will set right what was not right. This day, you will give your all." He sucked in a deep breath and let it out in a roar. "*We are the hammer*."

"*We are the hammer*," they roared back in answer.

Jax turned.

"Punch it."

The portal controller's hands once again danced on the console, and then inside the silver ring of the displacement machine, the air began to swirl and distort. There was a feeling of slight discomfort as the portal opened, and then like a magic trick, the swirling layer of oily distortion lengthened and dropped into a long, burning tunnel.

Jax walked to the front of his squad and held a hand aloft.

"For Germania and New Berlin." He pointed forward and began to run into the fiery tunnel.

CHAPTER 19

BERLIN – NORTHERN NEUKÖLLN – APARTMENT 3B

Heisen pushed through the small swing door to the kitchen and blew air through compressed lips at the sight of the pile of dirty dishes. The congealed food smelt like a blocked drain. He'd seen worse, much worse; one guy had drowned his cat in the sink, and then hung himself. After a week, they found him…and the cat. By then, the animal had turned into feline porridge and they needed full HAZMAT suits to even get near it.

Heisen guessed there were no clean cups, so grabbed one with the least amount of crap buildup and rinsed it out—he doubted a bit of extra bacteria was gonna kill the kid now. He shut the water off, turned, but then froze. The rim of the swing door glowed, and the smell of ozone filled the air. He stared at it, confused for a second or two, the half cup of water still in his hand.

It took him a few more seconds to guess what might be happening. A tingle of apprehension ran up his spine and he gently lowered the cup to the bench-top, crossed to the door, and eased it open a crack.

Klaus stood, hands up, as if surrendering to someone. He gibbered for a second or two, shaking his head until a tiny shaft of light struck him. The kid glowed for a moment, before falling backward. But before he even hit the ground, his body was collapsing into dust.

"*Fuck!*" Heisen felt a jolt run through him from his toes to his scalp. He pulled his Glock, sucked in a breath, and kicked the door open, immediately diving in and rolling. He came up fast, shooting at multiple targets. He missed every damn one of them.

A golden beam came out of nowhere, slicing through his shoulder and taking his gun arm. Then it all went to shit.

CHAPTER 20

THE DEFENSE – INTERACTION EVENT

Monroe held up a fist. Behind him, Raptor, Harper, Benson, Carter, and Felzig held their position and waited, focused just on him. They had cut the power to the building, throwing the old brownstone into darkness. Now each had L-3 Warrior NVGs—night vision goggles—pulled down over their eyes.

Monroe turned, his four electronic red-eyes taking in his team. He nodded and then turned back to the door. Its outline was clean and green-lit by the goggles—they were the latest tech, with two lenses pointed forward like traditional NVGs, giving him his hunter's depth perception, while two more tubes pointed slightly outward from the center to increase his peripheral view, allowing

Monroe and his team to more quickly move through the OODA loop—Observe, Orient, Decide, Act—all in a few seconds.

Monroe pointed two fingers at his team, then the door—Raptor moved fast, attaching a shaped charge to the door in a large X pattern. Then he attached a silver sheet from the top that unfurled covering the door—they wanted the entire wooden frame to be obliterated, out of their way, and most of the percussive blast to enter the room for maximum disorientation. Felzig had the EMP disc in her hand, rotated it, lights on its outside counting down as she held it ready.

Both agents got behind the wall to take cover. Monroe held up a hand, fingers splayed, and counted down, one finger at a time. He reached one and signaled the assault.

Whip-fast, Felzig slid the EMP disc under the door, immediately followed by Raptor triggering the breaching charge. The door exploded inward.

Monroe and his five-strong team charged in, their laser sights quickly finding the small goblin-like creatures scattering in the darkness. There would be no attempt to communicate, no compromise, no hostages. These things had come here to kill—brutally—Monroe's agents; the Defense would return the favor.

Monroe counted at least a dozen moving bodies, maybe more, when they came through. In seconds, they had adeptly halved that amount, even though the creatures seemed to be wearing body armor and moved agilely and quickly, like a cross between wolverines and deformed children.

Raptor took the center of the room, gun up and spitting rounds into the smoke-filled darkness, his laser sight picking out tiny bodies, and his unerring aim just as quickly putting them down.

Then it all changed. There came a high-pitched squeal from out of the dark, and then a yellow beam shot out to touch Raptor. The big man froze as a hole the size of a dinner plate opened in the front of his body. There was no wet-matter dispersal and no projectile follow-through, just an enormous hole burned clean through that didn't even bleed. Without a word, the big man fell backward like an oak tree.

Carter targeted the shooter, following its nimble movements as it scurried from position to position. But from his three o'clock another beam shot out. This time, there was no clean hole. Monroe watched as Carter's entire body shimmered where the golden beam touched and stayed on him. The man simply collapsed into a mound of powder before Monroe's eyes.

Monroe had to dive and roll as more of the deadly beams criss-crossed the room. He stopped with his back to an upturned table.

"Go to full auto," he roared and dived again, flicking the selector switch on his rifle and firing back at the source of the beams. Around him, his remaining agents changed up their delivery, moving out of the OODA loop and into a lethal spray mode—the intermittent coughs of the silenced weapons became a staccato beat as high-velocity rounds punched through anything they touched.

The remaining Defense members backed up, keeping each other out of the crossfire, targeting anything below waist level. Beams and bullets crossed in the small room. Monroe felt like they were fighting a pack of high-tech furies, so ferocious were the small beings in their resistance.

Felzig jumped over a couch, finding the downed detective. "Got the cop here," she yelled.

Monroe saw her go down on one knee and then reach down to brush the hair back off the guy's forehead, speaking softly to him.

He nodded, but didn't get up.

Felzig patted his chest, probably telling him to stay down, and then started to rapidly reload. But like magic, one of the small creatures appeared beside her in the smoke and pointed a small device up at her. She spun, but before she could react further, her face took the small beam front-on. Her entire head simply vanished, leaving a stump of neck seared dry.

Felzig stayed upright for a second or two, her arms dropping and then her body toppled onto the cop, who screamed and began to scrabble backward on one arm toward the window.

Monroe's teeth clenched, feeling the fury ball up in his chest. He liked Felzig. He'd fucked Felzig. She was a tough woman, an insatiable alley cat in the bedroom, and a tigress in the field. Now, she had simply ceased to exist—no scream of pain, no bleeding bullet wound or loud explosion, just a golden beam of light, and then...gone.

There was a low-level hum, and then he had a tingly feeling deep in his gut as the air in the closed space became oily and distorted. At the far side of the room, something that looked like a shimmering doorway opened.

From his position, Monroe saw a small figure disappear into it. The three-foot glowing oval was fixed to an external wall, and inside looked to be a long horizontal tunnel. Given there was a three-story drop on the other side of the wall, this doorway had to lead to somewhere other than thin air or Berlin street. Monroe remembered his initial code call: Non-Terrestrial Incursion.

Fuck that, he thought. *You aren't getting away that easy.*

He brought his gun up. "You think you're going home?" He sighted on the shimmering doorway and fired into it, emptying his magazine. Horns blared from somewhere deep inside it, and the portal snapped shut with a rush of charged air. "Fuck you. The rest of you are all mine." He ejected the empty magazine and snapped in another, yelling over his shoulder as he scanned the carnage in the room.

"Defense, count off."

From out of the dark, Benson and Harper yelled in return. But that was it.

Monroe waited, the smoke was settling, a broken window creating a small draft of clear air. There was a tinkle of falling glass, the sound of dripping water or blood, and soft moans of pain from the downed beings. He held his breath. Silence settled around him.

He slowly pulled off his NVGs and blinked once, his eyes quickly adjusting to the semi-gloom. In his peripheral vision, he detected a tiny movement, and snapped around to fire a single round at the small figure as it tried to improve its position in relation to him.

His bullet blew it off its feet, spinning it doll-like across the floor to land face down on the debris-strewn carpet.

"Cover."

Harper and Benson came up behind Monroe, facing away from him, scanning the room for movement. Monroe knelt to examine the creature. He kicked its weapon away, placed one huge boot on its back, and pressed down. It groaned. They were small, the same size as a three year old, but slim and perfectly formed except for their heads that were large. A helmet was pulled down over its face, and even though it looked to be wearing some sort of body armor, he saw that it was no match for the slug that had obliterated its shoulder.

He used the barrel of his gun to turn it over—it groaned again. He reached out and lifted the visor off its head. There was a rush of weird smelling air, and then a face from a nightmare. Monroe grimaced—it looked like a hairless, deformed child, with no nose, large eyes, and small shovel-like teeth. The skin looked transparent with pumping veins pushing dark blood into a large pulsating brain inside its potato-shaped head. It glared at him with a boiling hatred and revulsion that Monroe had never experienced before in his life.

One handed, he lifted the small being and stared into its face. His own features twisted in disgust. "What the fuck are you?"

There came a disgusted noise from the back of its throat and it bared its teeth. The eyes still burned into his own.

"Yeah, feeling's mutual, buddy." Monroe pointed the big gun at its face. "Got something for you from Felzig—open wide."

The small being began to smirk and reached up with its remaining good arm to punch a button on its belt.

"I'm Jax," it hissed at him. "It's clean-up time."

Monroe's eyebrows shot up. "So, you can talk."

A blinding light engulfed the small smashed body, then Monroe, then Benson and Harper, the room, and then the entire building.

In another moment, there was just a crater where the brownstone had stood for a hundred years.

EPILOGUE

A month later, Detective Heisen sat in a taxi across the road from the empty lot where the brownstone used to be. His eyes were glazed.

"What do you want to do, buddy?"

"*Huh*?" Heisen blinked at the sound of the driver's voice. "Give me a minute." He got out and crossed the road to stand at a sagging line of police tape still strung across the sidewalk—he didn't know what it was there for; there were no clues, never was to begin with. There was nothing to see and nothing to steal—nada, zero, zip—case closed.

He flipped up the tape and ducked under, groaning as the back-brace cut into his waist. He was out of work, pensioned off at thirty-eight—a one-armed detective with several separated discs in his back from the blast that had thrown him out the window that night.

At least that's what he'd been told. But he

knew that was bullshit. Truth was, there was no blast, and he had thrown himself out the window before the entire block of apartments had melted into nothing.

He was finished, as his injuries, along with the potential therapy for the rest of his life, didn't exactly make him Officer of the Year material.

His former squad hadn't been real supportive either: "that's the guy who saw hobbits, elves, and leprechauns," they'd sniggered.

Well, fuck 'em all. Heisen's curse turned into a groan; his salad days had turned to boiled cabbage nights in the blink of an eye.

Ed Heisen walked further in to stand in the center of the vacant lot. Beneath his feet, pumice-like material crunched. The boffins had told him that even the bricks, steel, everything, had been super-heated to a point of molecular transformation. He looked up, trying to judge where he had fallen from, trying to remember everything that happened, and what was real and what was the result of impacting with a sidewalk after a thirty-foot fall.

Heisen lifted his stump, staring for a moment. A gas explosion had been the official explanation. A gas explosion that had been as hot as a miniature sun neatly cut away his arm and cauterized the wound so cleanly that an industrial laser could not have been more efficient.

Heisen blew air through compressed lips. Nothing left but ghosts and memories. The agents, the Defense they had called themselves, had all vanished in the blast as well as the tiny creatures he knew existed. For all his digging, no reference to the special agents, to the tiny beings, to Klaus, or to the case was on file anywhere. Even Sergeant Amos had been reassigned and wouldn't take his calls. Someone way above even his superintendent's pay grade had shut this down and zipped it up so tight that even thinking about it was a dismissible offense.

This case had been buried and him along with it. No loose ends, nothing to see here, move along folks and enjoy your new life as a crippled ex-detective, Mr. Heisen.

The cab honked and he turned to wave.

But there was something they all forgot. He used to be a detective, and a damned good one. Agent Carter had said there was a strange radiation present—Xenon-135 he had called it.

Heisen reached into his pocket and pulled out a crumpled piece of brown paper with a name and address scrawled on it. With great difficulty, he opened it out with his remaining hand. He read it:

Professor Matthew Kearns, Harvard, Cambridge, Massachusetts.

Klaus had been determined to reach out to this academic for a reason, and even with Heisen's brief time he had before he was forced out of his job, his research found that for a linguistics professor, he was involved in some of the weirdest events imaginable.

Heisen bet that if anyone would believe his story and could trace Xenon-135, it would be Professor Matt Kearns. And if that material turned up again, then they were going to be there, waiting.

After all, everyone knows that if you capture a leprechaun it's good luck. He'd be waiting all right.

--- END ---

Made in the USA
San Bernardino, CA
21 June 2019